**Nell's dark gaze wa[...] little chin of hers was stubborn. He remembered taking it in his fingers, remembered how warm her skin had been and how silky it had felt.**

He met her gaze head-on. "I thought I told you that you weren't to contact me again."

"You did." She made another nervous adjustment to her coat. "And believe me, I wouldn't have done so. But..." A breath escaped her and she swallowed. "I need to tell you something."

He could smell her scent, sweet and tantalizing, and the fire in his chest seemed to burn brighter, hotter. He was going to be so late for Claire, but now that he was here in this elevator with Nell, he couldn't think of anything he wanted less than to leave and find a different woman. A woman who wasn't Nell.

*Remember why she's here.*

Ah, yes. There was that.

"Yes," Aristophanes said. "You're here to tell me you're pregnant."

# Scandalous Heirs

*Two impulsive nights of passion...*
*Two positive pregnancy tests!*

Billionaires and friends Cesare and Aristophanes
have both vowed never to let *anything* distract them
from their work. Distractions can only lead to ruin.
But neither can resist making the most dangerous
mistake of all—giving in to desire for two alluring
women. The consequences? Claiming their one-
night heirs!

Cesare is haunted by the memories of the mystery
woman he spent one night of passion with. Two
years later, they meet again in Italy by chance, and
he makes a shocking discovery—she's secretly had
his baby daughter, but she can't remember who he
is!

Read all about it in
*Italian Baby Shock*

When Aristophanes meets preschool teacher
Nell, they agree to one searing yet unforgettable
night together—no strings attached. Until he finds
her on his doorstep months later with a shocking
revelation... She's carrying his twins!

Find out more in
*The Twins That Bind*

Both available now!

# THE TWINS THAT BIND

## JACKIE ASHENDEN

Harlequin

**PRESENTS**

# Harlequin®
## PRESENTS™

Recycling programs for this product may not exist in your area.

ISBN-13: 978-1-335-93938-8

The Twins That Bind

Copyright © 2024 by Jackie Ashenden

Harlequin Enterprises ULC
22 Adelaide St. West, 41st Floor
Toronto, Ontario M5H 4E3, Canada
www.Harlequin.com

**Printed in Lithuania**

MIX
Paper | Supporting responsible forestry
FSC® C021394

**Jackie Ashenden** writes dark, emotional stories with alpha heroes who've just gotten the world to their liking only to have it blown apart by their kick-ass heroines. She lives in Auckland, New Zealand, with her husband, the inimitable Dr. Jax, two kids and two rats. When she's not torturing alpha males and their gutsy heroines, she can be found drinking chocolate martinis, reading anything she can lay her hands on, wasting time on social media or being forced to go mountain biking with her husband. To keep up-to-date with Jackie's new releases and other news, sign up to her newsletter at jackieashenden.com.

### Books by Jackie Ashenden

#### Harlequin Presents

*The Maid the Greek Married*
*His Innocent Unwrapped in Iceland*
*A Vow to Redeem the Greek*
*Spanish Marriage Solution*

#### Three Ruthless Kings

*Wed for Their Royal Heir*
*Her Vow to Be His Desert Queen*
*Pregnant with Her Royal Boss's Baby*

#### The Teras Wedding Challenge

*Enemies at the Greek Altar*

#### Scandalous Heirs

*Italian Baby Shock*

To all the heroes I give weird names to. Sorry (not).

# CHAPTER ONE

ARISTOPHANES KATSAROS, BILLIONAIRE owner of one of Europe's most influential financial companies, had every minute of his phenomenally expensive time planned down to the last second. His schedule was his bible, his compass, and if something wasn't in his schedule then it was irrelevant. He liked the certainty and he liked the control it gave him.

He was a man for whom control wasn't simply vital, it was a way of life.

So as he exited the gala he'd been attending in Melbourne, a dull affair that he didn't enjoy—social engagements were the bane of his existence—he checked his watch to make sure he was on time for the meeting he'd planned at the penthouse apartment he'd bought three years ago and never visited. A meeting he was sure would *not* be dull in the least.

Angelina was scheduled to join him for the night, as per his instructions to his personal secretary. She was tall, blonde, elegant, a professor of literature at an elite American college, and in Melbourne for a conference.

She, like he, had a very tight schedule and one night was all she could do.

Not that he minded.

He had a revolving schedule of lovers, women who wanted only a night and nothing more, and he liked to make sure he had at least a couple of evenings each week with one in whichever city he was in at the time.

Sex was necessary and it helped him let off steam, but he didn't prize it above anything else he had scheduled. It was a bodily requirement that he paid attention to as he paid attention to every bodily requirement in order to keep himself in optimum health.

He was looking forward to the evening, because he liked Angelina. She was cool, fearsomely intelligent and could more than hold her own in conversation with him. She was also uninhibited in bed and he was very much looking forward to that as well.

Beauty was not a requirement in his lovers, but intelligence was mandatory. Chemistry, too, was vital. His time was expensive and if he'd put aside the time for sex, then he wanted it. He also required that it should be as pleasurable as possible for all concerned.

That was all he was thinking as he came down the steps, his limo waiting for him at the kerb, and he wasn't paying any attention to the light drizzle coming down from the sky, or the slick stone of the footpath, or the small figure hurrying along said footpath.

Hurrying too fast, in retrospect.

Aristophanes had his phone out of his pocket and was in the process of texting Angelina that he was on his way, when he heard a cry and the sound of someone hitting pavement. He jerked his gaze from the screen, startled, only to see the small figure crumpled on the pavement directly in front of his limo.

It wasn't moving.

Aristophanes wasn't a man who acted without thinking. He considered all his options carefully. He took his time. But now, faced with an unmoving human being lying prone on a slick street, he didn't hesitate. He strode over and knelt on the wet stone, heedless of the rain on his immaculate black suit trousers.

The person was swathed in a cheap-looking black coat, what seemed to be miles of a woollen scarf, and he couldn't tell if it was a man or a woman until he'd managed to pull away all that fabric.

The loveliest woman he'd ever seen lay on the footpath in front of him.

For long moments he crouched there, ignoring the drizzle, almost transfixed.

She wasn't a conventional beauty, he supposed, though beauty didn't interest him the way it obsessed other people. He prized intelligence and self-control above all things, yet even he couldn't deny that the woman lying unconscious on the pavement was exceptionally pretty. Her features were delicate and precise, a small chin, finely arched brows, and the sweetest pout of a mouth. Thick, dark red lashes feathered her cheeks.

A couple of months ago he'd been forced to go to a gala at an art gallery in New York, and there had been an exhibition of Pre-Raphaelite painters. The gala had been as dull as expected so he'd busied himself by looking at the paintings instead, particularly those by Burne-Jones.

She reminded him of the women in those paintings. A Pre-Raphaelite beauty fallen on a wet pavement.

Not that he should be staring at her. She was unconscious, which meant she'd hit her head on said pavement, and what he should be doing was checking she was okay, not staring at her like a fool.

His driver had got out of the limo and was at his elbow, but Aristophanes didn't turn round. Instead he held a couple of fingers against the pale throat revealed by the plunging neckline of the black dress she was wearing. Her pulse beat strongly beneath her warm skin.

Thank God.

'Call an ambulance,' he said roughly to his driver. 'Now.'

He had other places to go tonight and this would put him behind schedule, but even he couldn't leave an unconscious woman lying on the pavement in the rain.

He stared down at her, frowning. The black dress she wore looked as cheap as her coat, but it clung to every curve, outlining a body made to fascinate a man for days. Full, luscious breasts, rounded hips, an elegant waist…and unless he was very much mistaken, she wasn't wearing any underwear.

A pulse of desire shot through him, making every muscle clench tight.

Disturbing. He'd never felt such an instant physical attraction to a woman before. He preferred conversation first before anything else, because it was always the mind that drew him, not the body.

But this woman's body...

He forced the thought away, hard. She was lying unconscious in the rain and he should be thinking about getting her warm, not noting her lack of undergarments.

Since moving her would be a mistake, he shrugged out of his handmade black cashmere overcoat instead, and laid it carefully over the top of her. She was so small the coat covered her.

'Ambulance is on its way, sir,' his driver said.

'Good.' Aristophanes didn't move from where he crouched beside the woman. 'Get an umbrella to shield her from the rain.'

The driver did so and, rather to his own surprise, Aristophanes found himself grabbing the umbrella from him, and holding it over the unconscious woman himself.

She was breathing, which was good, though she was very pale.

He checked his watch again. Time ticked by. The ambulance was coming. He could hear the siren. He should probably finish that text to Angelina to let her know he'd be delayed, yet he made no move to get his phone out. He kept holding the umbrella, crouched beside the woman, keeping the rain off her.

As the siren got louder, the woman made a soft sound and Aristophanes glanced down. Her eyelashes glowed reddish in the streetlights and were fluttering as she gave a moan. Instinctively, he put a hand on her shoulder to keep her still. Moving wasn't a good idea when the ambulance hadn't even arrived.

He'd never been a gentle man, never been one for kindness, but with an unconscious stranger on his hands, he made an attempt at both.

'Keep still,' he murmured. 'You have fallen and hit your head. An ambulance is coming.'

Her lashes fluttered again, then rose, revealing liquid dark eyes that met his unerringly. They were full of confusion and shock, and he wasn't sure what happened then, only it felt as if something large and solid had hit him squarely in the chest.

The ambulance sirens echoed.

He shook off the strange sensation and made as if to get to his feet—the paramedics would need room to work—but at that moment, a small hand crept out from under his coat and gripped his with surprising strength.

He froze.

Her eyes had closed again, but she didn't let go of his hand.

A long time ago, when he'd been on his fifth—or maybe his sixth?—foster family, he'd discovered a stray kitten underneath some stairs in the dusty concrete apartment block in Athens where he'd been living at the time. He'd been about twelve, or thirteen, and at that stage had still been bothering trying to make a connection with his current foster family. But his foster parents hadn't been interested, not when they'd had five other kids they were also fostering. So Aristophanes had been left to his own devices. Out of boredom and loneliness, he'd decided to adopt the kitten himself.

It had been wild, but he'd been patient, and eventually, using pilfered pieces of fish and crumbs of cheese, and little saucers of milk when he could get them, he'd got the kitten to begin to trust him. And the moment the kitten had allowed him to pick it up, he'd felt such a sense of achievement, as if there was something good about him after all.

It felt like that moment now, with this unknown woman clinging tightly to his hand. As if he were all that stood between her and destruction.

Aristophanes Katsaros was known as one of the brightest and best financial geniuses on the planet, and the financial algorithm he'd created had sent his fortunes into the stratosphere. He was a shark when it came to money, and numbers were his playground, his happy place. People, however, were far down on his list of priorities.

So he should have shaken her hand off, risen to his feet, and let the paramedics do their thing. Then he should have got into his limo and driven away to meet Angelina, and had the night of pleasure he'd allowed himself.

Except he didn't.

For no apparent reason that he could see, he stayed where he was, reluctant to pull his hand away from the small, slender fingers clutching his own. He couldn't recall a time anyone had reached for him, let alone some complete stranger in considerable distress.

Five minutes earlier, if anyone had told him that he'd be kneeling in the rain next to an unconscious woman and unable to pull away because she was holding his hand, he would have laughed.

Well, he might have laughed. If laughter were something he indulged in, which it wasn't. At the very least he would have ridiculed the idea.

Now, though, as the ambulance pulled up and the paramedics leapt out, he found himself staying exactly where he was, keeping hold of her hand. Eventually, he had to move though, so he eased his fingers from hers and stepped back to give the paramedics room to work.

It was time to go. Time send that text to Angelina and let her know that he was on his way.

But he didn't. He stood there, watching as the paramedics checked her over, shone a light into her eyes and murmured reassuringly to her.

She was awake again, her gaze darting around as if she was looking for someone.

Was it him? Though he couldn't think why she'd be looking for him, since she wouldn't know him from Adam. Still, he stepped closer and when she looked around again, her dark eyes met his. 'You,' she whispered and again reached out a hand to him.

The paramedics were putting her onto a wheeled stretcher and, once they'd strapped her in, he stepped in close and took her reaching fingers in his. They closed convulsively on his hand, gripping tight, and so he had no choice but to follow as they wheeled her to the ambulance.

'Will she be all right?' he asked one of the paramedics.

'She has a concussion,' the man said. 'We need to get her to hospital to get her checked out. Are you her next of kin?'

'No.' Aristophanes' attention was consumed by the woman and the grip she had on his hand. She felt so warm.

They were preparing to put her in the ambulance.

'I'm sorry, sir,' the paramedic said. 'If you're not her next of kin, you can't come with her.'

He hadn't planned on going with her. His plan for the evening was Angelina and her slender, supple body. Yet now the woman's grip tightened, as if she was trying to hold onto him, and he realised suddenly that he wouldn't be able to give his full attention to Angelina until he knew this complete stranger was okay.

She probably had next of kin somewhere, but she'd slipped over next to his limo and now he felt responsible. Also, she was holding onto his hand very tightly, making it clear—in his mind anyway—that she wanted his presence.

'I am coming with her,' he said flatly, using the same tone he always used when people disagreed with his wishes.

The paramedic shook his head. 'I'm sorry, sir. You can't.'

Aristophanes, who didn't hear the word no very often and never liked it when he did, focused on the man. 'I don't care.'

'Sir, you can't—'

'Yes, I can,' Aristophanes cut him off with all the force of his considerable authority. 'Or do you really want me to go to the trouble of buying your hospital just so I can fire you?'

The paramedic opened his mouth. Shut it. Then shrugged and muttered something Aristophanes decided not to catch.

They loaded the woman into the ambulance and let Aristophanes climb in beside her, and he continued to hold her hand as the sirens started and they sped towards the hospital.

She sighed, settling on the stretcher, her eyes closing.

Angelina was going to have to wait.

Nell was having a lovely dream. She'd been running from something very upsetting and had fallen over, and then the most beautiful man she'd ever seen had grabbed her hand to help her up. He was holding onto it now and she didn't want to let him go. She didn't want to let him go ever. He was so strong and reassuring and she was sure that nothing could touch her while he was here.

Now they were dancing and…no…wait…they couldn't be dancing because she was lying down and not moving, and her head was hurting, and she felt dizzy. Had she been drinking? Had she got really, really drunk?

Then again, no, she couldn't be drunk because she didn't drink much and, anyway, she had work the next day and she never missed work. She loved her job at the preschool, and she loved the kids. So not drunk, then. Perhaps she was sick and that was why her head was hurting?

If felt like an effort to open her eyes, but she managed it, expecting to find herself in her little flat in Brunswick with the morning light coming through the window.

Except she wasn't in her bed or in her flat.

She was lying on what looked like a hospital bed with a curtain drawn around it, and someone was holding her hand.

Wait, what? A hospital bed? What on earth was she doing in hospital?

Desperately she tried to remember what had happened. Things were a little hazy, but she'd got to the bar where she was supposed to meet Clayton—she'd been seeing him for about a month—and had sat there waiting for him. She'd dressed up specially, because she'd decided that tonight was the night she was going to sleep with him. She hadn't yet, wanting to wait until she was sure he was someone she could see having a long-term relationship with, and only in the past couple of weeks had she decided that, yes, he was.

So she'd worn a slinky black dress that clung to her generous curves and, in a fit of daring that wasn't like her at all, she hadn't put on any underwear. He'd been getting impatient with their lack of physical contact, so she'd wanted to make sure he knew that she was ready and willing right now.

Except then he hadn't turned up. At first she'd thought he was just late. But then late had turned into *very* late, and then, an hour after that, she'd got a text from him saying he was sorry, but he didn't think this would work between them. She was too uptight, he'd said, too many hang-ups about sex, which wasn't what he was looking for.

After the text, she'd walked out of the bar into the drizzly night, upset and full of embarrassment that she'd put on a sexy dress and no underwear for a man who hadn't wanted her. Who in the end had left her to wait in the bar for an hour then not even turned up.

She'd been determined not to cry as she'd walked blindly through the drizzle and then...something had happened and she'd woken up here.

At that moment someone bent over her and she found herself looking up into a pair of eyes the dark grey of thunderclouds, framed by long black lashes and straight black brows.

Her breath caught.

It was the man. The beautiful man from her dream. Except apparently he wasn't a dream after all.

His face was all rough angles and chiselled planes, his mouth hard, his cheekbones high, and he had the most impressive jaw she'd ever seen.

No, perhaps beautiful wasn't the right word for him. Compelling, maybe. Or magnetic.

Electric.

Nell stared at him, her voice vanishing somewhere she couldn't reach.

He was very tall, wide shoulders and broad, muscled chest encased in an expertly tailored white shirt that looked somewhat damp. He also wore black trousers that highlighted a narrow waist and powerful thighs and…

Lord. What was she doing? She never gazed at men like that. She'd certainly never gazed at Clayton like that. Then again, Clayton didn't look like this man and, also, Clayton had ghosted her in a bar the night she'd planned on sleeping with him.

Clayton, who she'd thought was the perfect man for her. Who worked for a bank, owned his own home, and was good-looking. Whom she'd had fun with and—

*And who didn't want you.*

Nell swallowed, a hot wave of remembered embarrassment washing through her, but she forced the thought away, concentrating instead on the man at her bedside and not the man who'd left her high and dry.

He looked expensive, this man in his damp evening clothes, and he radiated authority, as if he were one of the doctors who ruled this ER. No, as if he were one of the people who ruled the entire hospital, or possibly even the entire city itself. Maybe even the whole country…

Then something else interrupted the rush of chaotic thoughts. He was holding her hand, his fingers warm and strong, and somehow reassuring. She wanted to tighten her grip, as if he were all that stood between her and a hundred-foot drop.

'Are you well?' His voice was deep and a touch rough, with a hint of an accent she couldn't place. Definitely not Australian.

Nell tried to find her own. 'Um… My head hurts.'

'Yes,' the man said. 'You had an accident. You slipped

on the wet pavement and hit your head, and so I called an ambulance. You are in hospital.'

Oh, God. She must have been more upset than she'd thought if she'd slipped. She was normally pretty careful on the bluestone paving of Melbourne's streets, especially when it was raining. It had better not be serious. Sarah, her manager, would be extremely annoyed if she couldn't go to work the next day, since they were already short-staffed.

At that moment the curtain was pushed back and a doctor came in, looking harried. 'Miss Underwood,' she said. 'How are you feeling?'

'A bit woozy,' Nell replied.

'Of course, you've had quite the knock on the head. Luckily, Mr Katsaros here was able to call an ambulance and get you in to see us.'

'It was nothing,' the man—Mr Katsaros—said dismissively. He released his grip on her hand and glanced at her. 'You'll be looked after here.'

Her fingers tingled from where he'd been holding them, and his grey gaze was very sharp, very intense. It was as if all the air in the room had been sucked away when he looked at her, which was disconcerting.

'Thank you,' she said, trying to sound her usual calm, firm self since that was her default setting whenever she was disconcerted. Being calm and firm also worked extremely well with small children, animals and overbearing men.

'We'll need to do a brief examination,' the doctor

said, 'but first I need to know if you have anyone at
home who can look after you.'

Nell swallowed, her mouth a little dry. 'No, I live
alone.'

'Friends or family?'

She shook head again. The only friend she could call
on was Lisa, who also worked at the preschool, but she
was on holiday in Bali. And as for her family... Her
parents had died when she was a child, and there was
no point asking her aunt or uncle. Or her cousins. She
hadn't been in contact with them for years and didn't
know how to reach them even if she'd wanted to. Which
she didn't. They'd never been interested in her and the
feeling was mutual.

The doctor frowned. 'You need to be with someone
for at least twenty-four hours. Are you sure you don't
have anyone you can call?'

Nell's head was starting to feel a little better so she
sat up, taking it slow, pleased to find the dizziness re-
ceding. 'I'm sure I'll be fine,' she said. There was her
neighbour, Mrs Martin, who could look in on her. No
need to put anyone else to any trouble over a silly bump
on the head. 'I have a neighbour who can—'

'I will look after you,' Mr Katsaros interrupted unexpectedly, his voice like stone, heavy with authority.

Nell blinked.

He'd turned to look at her again, his dark grey eyes
boring into hers, radiating that peculiar intensity that
sent a hot, electric feeling through her. It was disturbing. *He* was disturbing.

Rattled, she dredged up a sunny yet impersonal smile. 'Thank you. That's a very kind offer, but I couldn't possibly put you to the trouble.'

His gaze remained unblinking, making her feel as if she were a specimen on a slide put under a very powerful microscope. 'It is no trouble.'

The electric feeling intensified, which disturbed her even more, so she smiled harder. 'As I said, it's very kind of you, but…well. You're a complete stranger and I have no idea who you are.'

'Aristophanes Katsaros,' he said without hesitation, as if he'd been waiting hours for her to ask. 'Google me.'

The doctor, who was checking her phone and now looking even more harried, glanced at Nell. 'I need to do a few checks before we can let you go, Miss Underwood. But I can't release you if you don't have anyone to be with you.'

The pain in Nell's head receded to a dull ache. 'As I said, I have a neighbour who can—'

'You will be in no danger,' the preposterously named Aristophanes Katsaros interrupted yet again, that storm-grey gaze not moving from hers. 'Not from me. I have a doctor on my staff who can keep an eye on you.'

At that moment an alarm sounded from somewhere beyond the curtain around her bed, and people began shouting. The doctor pulled a face, then vanished back out through the curtain without another word.

Clearly some emergency was happening.

Mr Katsaros didn't move, making the confined space seem even smaller than it was already, filling it with a tense, kinetic energy that made her heart beat hard. And it wasn't with fear. She didn't know what it was.

'I'm sorry,' she said, going into firm teacher mode automatically. 'But I don't know you from a bar of soap. And while I'm grateful for you coming to my rescue, I don't understand why you'd suddenly want to spend the next twenty-four hours looking after me.'

He stared down at her from his great height, standing quite still and yet somehow making the air around him vibrate with that strange electricity. His gaze flicked along the length of her body stretched out on the bed then came back to her face, the dark storm grey turning to silver. 'Do you have anyone else?'

Abruptly, she became conscious that her slinky black dress was damp and clinging to every single curve she had and that...oh, yes, she wasn't wearing underwear.

Her cheeks burned. How bloody mortifying. Here she was in this stupid dress that she'd put on for Clayton, with no underwear, lying in hospital because she'd knocked herself out. And this man had rescued her. He likely already knew what she had on underneath, or rather what she *didn't* have on underneath. What must he think of her?

Nell wanted to grab a blanket and pull it over herself, hide away from this far too magnetic man's gaze, but there wasn't one. All she could do was brazen it out, pretend she was wearing a suit of armour instead of a layer of cheap black jersey.

She gave him a very direct, quelling look. 'I've already said I have a neighbour.'

'Will they be able to stay with you the entire time?' he asked. 'A head injury can be very dangerous.'

Nell gritted her teeth. He was being very…insistent and she couldn't fathom why. The real problem, though, was that Mrs Martin, her neighbour, was eighty-five and had a bad hip. She used a walker, too, and, while Nell thought she could manage to pop in a couple of times over the course of twenty-four hours, Nell certainly couldn't ask her to stay.

Which meant Nell was in a difficult position.

She stared at Aristophanes Katsaros, who stared back intently, silver glittering in his eyes. It made her skin feel tight, that look, made her feel restless in a way she couldn't pinpoint. As if she were excited or thrilled by the way he looked at her, which couldn't be right. Why would she be excited about that?

*Clayton never looked at you that way.*

No, he hadn't. He'd been patient with her at first when she'd refused to sleep with him, telling her that it was fine, he'd wait. But then he'd been less patient, more irritated, making vague comments about his 'needs' and wasn't she being a little selfish?

Anger flickered at the memory and, briefly, she thought about lying to the demanding Mr Katsaros, but a lie involving a head injury would be very stupid and she wasn't stupid.

'No,' she said with a bit of bite in her tone. 'No, they will not be able to stay with me the entire time.'

'In that case you will come with me.' He said it as if that were the most logical thing in the world.

'I don't know you from—'

'Google me.'

'But I—'

'Do it.' He handed her his phone, his gaze relentless. 'I'll wait.'

His insistence made her bristle. 'Forgive me, but I'm not sure why you're insisting on looking after a complete stranger. I can arrange my own babysitter, believe me.'

His straight black brows drew together slightly, but the intense look in his eyes didn't waver. 'You slipped beside my car. You are my responsibility, and I take my responsibilities very seriously.'

A pulse of inexplicable heat went through her, though she wasn't sure why. She didn't want to be his responsibility. She'd been other people's responsibility for years after her parents' deaths, and it hadn't turned out that well, at least not for her.

Clearly impatient with her silence, he nodded at the phone. 'Search my name.'

Nell was tempted to tell him very firmly that he couldn't tell her what to do, but that wasn't going to help matters and, anyway, she abhorred a fuss.

Reluctantly, she opened the web browser in the sleek black piece of technology in her hand.

'Do you need me to spell it?' he asked.

She gave him a look. 'Aristophanes. Like the ancient Greek playwright?'

'Yes.'

'Fine.'

'Katsaros is spelled K-A-T—'

'I can manage,' she said coolly, interrupting him for a change as she entered his surname—it was Greek, she thought—into the web browser.

Hundreds of hits came up. Newspaper articles, magazine articles, think pieces, opinion posts, essays, interviews, videos… A bewildering array of information about Katsaros International, a huge finance company, and its mathematical-genius founder, who'd invented a financial algorithm that did something to the stock market.

Aristophanes Katsaros was that powerful billionaire founder, and he was currently standing at her hospital bedside in the busy ER of a public hospital, staring at her as if he wanted to eat her alive.

*You would like him to.*

The pulse of heat became a flame flickering inside her, and she couldn't keep telling herself that she didn't know what it was, not this time.

It was physical attraction, pure and simple.

She didn't understand. Why on earth would she be attracted to this stranger? She didn't know anything about him and, given how insistent and overbearing he seemed to be, she wasn't sure she'd like him even if she did. There was no way on earth she could be *attracted* to him. Yet, she couldn't deny that she felt hot when he looked at her, restless too, a million ants under her skin.

She'd had a grand total of one lover in her life and Clayton was to be the second, but even Clayton had never made her feel like this. That was the issue. Clayton had made her feel…well…nothing. If this was indeed attraction, and she'd never felt it before so she wasn't entirely sure, then Clayton hadn't made her feel even a tenth of what Aristophanes Katsaros made her feel.

Bewildering. She didn't like it. She *wouldn't* like him to eat her alive, and what she actually wanted was to be out of his disturbing, electric presence.

Also, she didn't need him to make such a fuss. If he was indeed the founder of Katsaros International, then he had much better things to be doing than looking after a lowly preschool teacher. Why on earth was he making all this effort for her?

'I see,' she said after a moment, gripping her self-possession as tightly as she could. 'May I ask why?'

His straight dark brows twitched again. 'What do you mean why?'

She gestured at the phone. 'You're very rich and obviously very important. Why on earth would you waste time looking after me?'

'Waste time…' he echoed, looking puzzled, as if the words meant nothing to him. 'No, you do not understand. I never waste time. Every second is accounted for, and I can assure you that I have rearranged my schedule to account for looking after you.'

Nell blinked. He had a strange way of speaking, as if his words were precious and he was doling them out one at a time. His accent was tantalising though, making soft music out of his deep voice, making her want to hear him speak again just for the pleasure of it.

Still…he'd rearranged his schedule? For her? Why would he do that?

She stared at him blankly, not knowing what to say.

Apparently, though, he didn't need her to say anything, because he checked the heavy-looking watch on his left wrist then reached for his phone, plucking it out of her hand. He glanced down at the screen and began to type one-handed, his thumb moving deftly.

'I will have you examined by my doctor. It will be quicker,' he said, still typing. 'It is pointless to wait further here.'

Nell opened her mouth in an automatic protest, but then he lifted the phone and spoke into it in a language that wasn't English. Maybe Greek, given his last name? He was short, to the point and devastatingly authoritative, before ending the call abruptly. 'Come,' he ordered, holding out a hand to her. 'I have my doctor waiting.'

The air of authority with which he spoke, as if the world were his to command, shocked her. She'd never met anyone with such a sense of their own importance.

Well. He might be a very famous, very rich, very powerful billionaire, while she was only a preschool teacher who was neither rich, famous nor particularly powerful, but she still wasn't going to go with him just because he said so.

'I don't care who you have waiting,' Nell said with the same gentle firmness she used with particularly recalcitrant children. 'But I'm not going with you and that's final. As I keep saying, I have a neighbour who can—'

'I don't care about your neighbour.' He didn't take his gaze from hers. 'Do you know how serious a head injury can be, Miss Underwood? The paramedic explained it to me on the way to hospital. You might feel fine now, but you could have a blood clot or any one of a number of serious complications. He was very clear that some-one needs to be with you for the next twenty-four hours. So unless you fancy a hospital stay, in which case you'll be taking a bed from someone who might need it more than you do, I suggest coming with me now.'

# CHAPTER TWO

ARISTOPHANES WAS VERY conscious of the seconds ticking by, of the further rearrangements in his schedule he might need to make. He'd already wasted hours at the hospital and he did not want to waste any more. His assistants had organised his doctor and his doctor had begun the process of handling the hospital bureaucracy. She would meet him at the penthouse apartment. Everything was being handled. There was nothing money and power couldn't arrange for him if he required it.

However, apparently the one thing his money and power couldn't arrange was Miss Underwood's consent to go with him, and she was currently being difficult. It was annoying. While he hadn't expected her to fall in with his wishes immediately, he'd thought she might take one look at his Wikipedia page and *then* graciously agree.

But she had not. What she'd given him was a look of brief shock, then, to his surprise, had doubled down on her refusal.

He found that inconceivable.

He wasn't a household name, it was true, but most

people, in his experience, knew who he was. Knew the story of the company he'd started building when he was a teenager, already playing the stock market with his frugal earnings from a job in an Athens fast-food outlet.

He hadn't gone to university. He'd found school dull and had left as soon as he could, which had been at fourteen. Numbers had been his delight, his music, and he'd created symphonies with them. He made money obey his every wish, doubling, tripling, moving from place to place, fluid as water. Sometimes he lost it, but that didn't matter, because he could always make more and he did. Effortlessly.

People called him a genius, but for him that was merely the way he was. As long as he kept to his schedule. Time was money. Seconds were euros that he poured into something productive, because if he wasn't productive, he was nothing. And he couldn't be nothing. He'd been nothing once before, to the woman who'd called herself his mother and yet who'd never been any kind of mother to him. She'd taken him to church with her when he was eight, and then after the service she'd told him to sit still and be quiet and then she'd left. Without him.

He'd still been sitting there an hour later when the priest had found him. They'd searched for his mother for days, but she was long gone by then. That had been the beginning of his climb from the nothingness of being abandoned, and he would never allow anything like that to happen to him again.

Now this lovely little woman was sitting up in the hospital bed, staring at him with those dark, dark eyes, her delicate features set in stubborn lines, and she seemed to be hell-bent on wasting his time with her arguments. Yet all he could think about was not his wasted hours, minutes and seconds, but how beautiful she was. How she irritated him with her refusals and how mystified he was that he cared so much about them.

Possibly he was irritated because of the constant ache of physical lust that dragged at him whenever he looked at her, which had never happened to him before. Not without a meeting of minds first. He resented it. She was a complete stranger to him, he knew nothing of her mind and how it worked, and that was not the usual order of things for him. It further irritated him that he couldn't understand why he felt that way, either.

A fascinating mind was of the utmost importance to him, and then physical attraction. The chemistry of bodies was nothing compared to the intrigue of how a woman thought. But he had no idea how Nell Underwood thought. What he wanted was her body.

Annoyed with himself and his physical feelings, he stared stonily back at her. He just couldn't understand why she was protesting. She'd read his history; it was all there in black and white on the Internet. He wasn't a serial killer or an axe murderer. She had nothing to fear from him, so why was she arguing? Yes, he was a stranger, but he was hardly some random passer-by.

He was Aristophanes Katsaros. One of the richest men in the world. Some would argue that rich men weren't exactly pure as the driven snow and that maybe she was right to be apprehensive of him. But he'd never hurt a woman in his entire life and he wasn't about to start. That wouldn't be a productive use of his time anyway.

Tonight, his body had expected sex and that was still his plan—Angelina had some work to do and she hadn't minded waiting—but he needed to make sure Miss Nell Underwood was taken care of. His doctor would keep her under observation for the requisite number of hours. It would not be a problem.

Her cheeks had flushed prettily and he found his gaze drawn yet again to the deliciously feminine lines of her body. There were no bra lines, no panty lines showing under the cheap, clinging black jersey. She wasn't wearing a stitch beneath it, and he was inexplicably intrigued by that. Where had she been going wearing no underwear? Was she a sex worker? A high-end escort? Had she been going to meet a lover?

He didn't understand why he wanted to know. He didn't understand why her body fascinated him. Because it wasn't as if he didn't know what a woman looked like naked. He knew very well about breasts and hips and the soft, wet, hot place between a woman's legs.

Yet it seemed to him as if he was intrigued by *this* woman and *her* body, and he wasn't sure why. All bodies were the same and they all worked the same, too, but it was the mind that was different. It was the mind that fascinated him.

'No,' she said, calm yet firm. 'I don't think so. Your doctor can come to me instead.'

Her voice was huskier than expected and it stroked

over his skin in a velvet caress. He wanted to hear it again. He wanted to hear it moaning his name as he made her come, as he—

Aristophanes gritted his teeth, dragging his thoughts away from that particular track.

No wasn't acceptable. He didn't like. He didn't like being unable to fathom why his body wanted her so very badly. And he *really* didn't like that a part of him didn't want to let her go. A part of him felt that she was his obligation now, his responsibility. Absurd to liken a woman to the kitten he'd once rescued, but still, that was how he felt. He'd witnessed her getting hurt and he'd looked after her until the ambulance came. She'd reached for his hand, had held it as if she hadn't wanted to let him go and yet apparently now his doctor was preferable to him.

Logically it made sense, so why was he feeling the need to argue with her? His doctor would be there, his sense of obligation duly discharged. He didn't need to be there himself, and besides, the longer he stayed, the more the seconds poured through his fingers, becoming minutes, turning to hours, time sliding away into nothing.

He had places to go, people to see. This strange fascination with her had already cost him a few hours of his evening and he didn't want it to cost any more.

Yet as she sat there in the hospital bed, he found his gaze returning yet again to her delicious curves. Full breasts, the perfect dip of her waist, rounded hips to grip and grip tight. That glorious mane of thick auburn hair, long enough to wind around his wrist to tug her mouth close. And her mouth… Yes, there were so many things he could do with that beautiful, full mouth…

Her eyes went wide and she tore her gaze away, her skin flushing the most beautiful shade of pink.

She'd seen what was in his eyes. She'd seen the hunger there. He'd betrayed himself, which was unconscionable, and yet still a part of him had noted the blush in her cheeks, the racing pulse at the base of her throat.

He wasn't the only one who'd betrayed themselves.

*You should go. Now.*

He gave a soundless growl. Yes, he should. If she didn't want him there, that was fine. He wouldn't insist. He had Angelina to quench the curious flare of desire that had sprung to life inside him, and she was always appreciative of his attention. He wanted more from his partners than just sex anyway. Sex was easy and cheap and he disdained easy and cheap. Sex could be had from anyone. Time was precious, so why would he spend it satisfying only his body, when he could also satisfy his mind?

He would have his night with Angelina and he would forget about Miss Nell Underwood.

'Very well,' he said coldly. 'If that's what you prefer. Give me your address and I will have my doctor escort you home.'

She did and then he forced himself to leave her bedside and wait for his doctor away from her.

Things moved with their usual smoothness after that. His doctor arrived, leaving Aristophanes to finally go to the penthouse apartment he owned, where Angelina was waiting for him, and once there, he should have forgotten about Miss Nell Underwood completely.

But he didn't. He couldn't.

His normal plan for an evening with a lover was an excellent meal, a very good glass of wine, an interesting conversation and then some mutually satisfying sex.

However, when he got to the apartment, the meal his favourite chef had prepared was lukewarm, the wine subpar, and Angelina irritated at being made to wait. Then, to make matters even worse, he couldn't stop thinking about the woman he'd left back in the hospital ER. His brain kept reminding him of the shape of her body underneath that clinging dress, and the way her gorgeous auburn hair had curled in the rain. How soft her mouth had looked. How she'd gripped his hand so tightly, as if she couldn't bear to let go of him. How, after she'd fallen, her beautiful deep brown eyes had opened and he'd looked into them and felt something deep and profound shift inside him.

He was furious. His evening plans had been blown to smithereens and it was all her fault.

Angelina, sensing his distraction, tried her best to engage him. He'd been neglecting his sexual needs for a couple of months because he'd been fine-tuning an update to his algorithm and when business called, he was consumed by it. So his body should have been primed and ready for sex from the moment he'd walked into his apartment. But when Angelina kissed him and he prepared for the usual rush of lust, there was nothing. And when she ran a hand down the front of his trousers, caressing him through the fabric, he didn't get hard. Even when he kissed her back and slid his palm down her spine, touching her skin…

He felt nothing.

His body wanted sex, but not with Angelina. His body wanted the Burne-Jones angel he'd left in the ER, and it didn't care what his mind wanted.

Aristophanes had never been turned inside out by physical desire. He was always in complete control of himself physically and emotionally, because only then could he set his mind free. The body and its needs were an inconvenience that he tolerated and managed accordingly, but this… He could not tolerate this and most especially not when he didn't even understand why she'd got so completely and thoroughly under his skin.

Which meant that there was only one thing he could do.

The answer to his problem didn't lie with Angelina.

It lay with Miss Nell Underwood.

And fortunately, he had her address.

Mr Katsaros' doctor was nice and a complete professional, much to Nell's annoyance, since she didn't want to like anything associated with the disturbing, kind of rude, yet also mesmerising man who'd left her in the ER.

The doctor gave her a thorough examination, before dealing with the hospital paperwork. Then a car arrived for them, delivering them back at Nell's small but cosy flat in Brunswick.

Nell, going automatically into hostess mode, tried to make the doctor some tea, but was then told in no uncertain terms that the correct behaviour after a knock to the head was rest.

That was annoying too, because she wasn't good with rest. She liked to be doing something, so, instead of going into her bedroom and lying down, she went to have a hot shower. She was cold, her head ached, and she wanted to get out of her damp dress.

She also felt oddly...abandoned.

Aristophanes Katsaros had left her in the ER. After first arguing with her, then staring at her as if he wanted to eat her alive, he'd agreed to her wishes without another protest before turning around and leaving.

And she'd felt deflated, which was ridiculous because what more had she expected? If he truly was who he'd said he was, then why on earth would he want to stay in the ER with her? She was merely a random stranger that he'd helped, and he'd already helped as much as he'd been able to. There wasn't anything more he could do.

Yet still, her heart pinched tight at the memory of his powerful figure disappearing through the curtains around her bed. He hadn't looked back and she hadn't realised she'd wanted him to until he didn't.

It was the way he'd looked at her just before he'd left that was the issue. His gaze burning bright silver as it followed the line of her body before coming to rest on her face once again. She knew what a man wanted when he looked at a woman that way. Clayton had looked at her in a similar way, yet his gaze had never been as hot, never been as hungry. And more importantly, she'd only felt…warm in return. Warm, not burning hot. A bit peckish, not starving. Pleased that he wanted her, of course, yet…

If she was being really honest with herself, she'd never felt the rush of sudden, hot physical desire for Clayton. Had never been so breathless in his presence that all thought had left her head. Never felt as if her cheeks were on fire whenever he'd caught her looking at him. In fact, she couldn't remember looking at him the way she'd looked at Aristophanes Katsaros.

God, it was stupid to be thinking about him. It didn't matter how he looked at her. He was too disturbing for her peace of mind anyway, and she should be glad he'd walked away.

Peeling off the embarrassing, ridiculous dress, Nell stepped into the shower, sighing as warm water ran over her chilled skin. Apart from a painful lump at the back of her skull, the ache in her head had receded and she was feeling a lot better. The doctor had given her a list of concussion symptoms to watch for and Nell was to let her know if she felt woozy or dizzy. Some people didn't develop concussion, though, so she might be fine, especially if she'd only been out for a couple of seconds.

Nell wasn't sure how long she'd been unconscious, but she had none of the symptoms the doctor had mentioned. Maybe she'd be one of the ones who didn't develop any. She hoped so. She didn't want to annoy Sarah by not coming into work tomorrow.

Once she'd showered, she stepped out of the stall and

dried herself off, then reached for the thick pink fluffy robe she always wore when it was cold, wrapping herself up in it. Humming softly, she towel-dried her hair to get most of the water out before winding the towel around her head turban-style.

Then she opened the bathroom door, stepped out into the hall, and came to a dead stop.

A man stood in the middle of her tiny, narrow hallway.

A familiar man.

Aristophanes Katsaros.

All the breath left her body in a wild rush, an electric thrill shooting straight through her, and her first thought was, *Thank God*. He hadn't abandoned her after all. He'd come back.

He stood with his arms folded across his muscular chest, filling the hall with his compelling physical presence. His height and the broad width of his shoulders, the flickering silver fire in his storm-grey eyes. A crackling energy seemed to leap between them, rooting her to the spot.

He seemed to be furious about something and, given the way he was looking at her, that something appeared to be her.

Her mouth became a desert. She had no idea what he was doing here.

'I have dismissed the doctor.' His deep rough voice was a shock to her system, as if she'd been fast asleep and the sound of it had woken her up. 'I said you were my responsibility and so you are. For the next twenty-four hours.'

She struggled to find her own voice. 'But…why? Don't you have better things to do?'

'I did.' His gaze slid over her and she was very aware that she was naked underneath her fluffy pink robe and…oh, yes, she was wearing a fluffy pink robe. And a towel turban. Sexy. 'Until you interrupted my evening with your accident.'

There was definite accusation in his tone and her cheeks heated. She was shocked he was here, embarrassed to be caught in her dressing gown with a towel around her head, and already angry with herself for thinking about him. Him getting angry with her for having the gall to slip in front of him was the last thing she needed.

'I'm terribly sorry your evening was inconvenienced by my head injury,' she snapped. 'I'll be sure to watch my step better next time when incredibly rude, overbearing men are in my vicinity.'

His black brows twitched again, his gaze sharpening. 'I am *not* overbearing.'

'Really? Then maybe I imagined you flinging your phone at me and ordering me to google you. I probably imagined you ordering me to come with you back to your residence, and being petulant when I refused, too.'

He said nothing, yet she could see the temper glittering in his eyes.

She shouldn't have spoken to him that way. Why had she? She was always patient, always caring and considerate. Never rude. It was just… Everything about him rattled her.

Still, she handled some of the worst nonsense humanity was capable of every day in the form of four-year-olds. She would not let a confrontation with one adult man get the better of her.

Nell lifted her chin, determined to show him that she was not intimidated by him and his silly little male temper, not one bit.

He glowered, obviously unimpressed by this show of defiance. 'Do you know what I had planned for this evening?' he bit out.

'No.' Nell lifted her chin even higher, ignoring how her heart beat far too fast and her skin was tight and hot. 'I can't imagine how your evening plans would be at all relevant to me.'

He did not like this one bit, something hot leaping in his eyes, and he took a step towards her, his arms still folded, his stare relentless. 'Sex, Miss Underwood. That's what I had planned for my evening. Dinner, conversation and sex. But because I couldn't stop thinking about you, I could not pay proper attention to my date.'

'That sounds like a you problem,' she said coolly. 'I didn't ask you to come here, Mr Katsaros, and if you're so concerned about your date, perhaps you should be with her instead of standing in my hallway being annoyed with me. Certainly you'll get more sex that way.'

His glower turned into a scowl and she *really* didn't like how hot that made her feel. As if part of her was pleased she was getting under his skin as much as he was getting under hers.

'I *tried* being with my date,' he growled. 'It didn't work.'

'Inside voice, please,' she said automatically.

'Excuse me?'

Nell knew a moment's fierce embarrassment as she realised what she'd said, then shoved it away. He couldn't blame her for treating him like a four-year-old when he was acting like one.

'It's what I tell the children in my preschool class,' she said, meeting his hot gaze head-on. 'When they are throwing tantrums.'

For a second something tense and electric crackled in the air between them.

'Your preschool class,' he echoed as if he'd never heard of such a thing.

'That's right.' She didn't look away. 'I'm a preschool teacher.'

'Good God,' he muttered with some disgust. 'Then what is the point of all of...*this*?' He flung out a hand, clearly indicating her.

Nell stiffened. 'All of what? What are you talking about?'

'All of you.' He virtually spat the words. 'You are the most beautiful woman I've ever seen and I have not been able to stop thinking about you since I left you in the ER.'

Nell blinked. No one ever complimented her. Clayton had told her she was pretty a couple of times when they'd first started going out, but then the compliments had stopped, and he'd started complaining about her more than he'd praised her. And as for her aunt and uncle, who'd taken her in after her parents had died... They hadn't complimented her either. They'd been resentful they'd had to look after her in the first place, and had made no secret of the fact.

Yet now this maddening man had called her beautiful and seemed to regard this as a personal affront, and she didn't know whether to be complimented or insulted.

'Fine,' she said, struggling to hold onto a patience that was usually limitless. 'You're upset about the interruption to your evening and I'm truly sorry about that.' She wasn't and made sure that her tone indicated that she wasn't. 'I'm also sorry my appearance is such an aggravation. But you really don't have to stay.' She gave him one of the sunny smiles that always cheered the children she taught. 'I'll be fine. So why don't you go off and have your little evening, and enjoy your date, hmm?' She'd wanted to sound calm, firm and authoritative. Yet she had a horrible suspicion that the words that had escaped were the ones she'd usually use with Dylan, one of the naughtiest boys in her class. Dylan. Who was four.

Aristophanes Katsaros, who was definitely not four, stared at her as if he couldn't believe what she'd said. 'My little evening?' he repeated. 'My *little* evening?' He took another step forward, and then another, and another, stalking down the hallway towards her, and

Nell found herself backing up and up, until the closed door of her bedroom was hard at her back, stopping her.

He towered over her, so much bigger and more powerful than she was. If he decided to do anything to her, she wouldn't stand a chance. She should have been terrified.

Yet she wasn't. She was…exhilarated almost. This man was a billionaire. The founder of a huge company. He was a mathematical genius and he hadn't been able to stop thinking about her. He'd dismissed the doctor so he could look after her. He'd said she was the most beautiful woman he'd ever seen.

Yes, he seemed angry about that, but he'd also called an ambulance when she'd been unconscious and injured. He'd held her hand and come to the hospital with her.

He wasn't going to do anything to her; she knew that as well as she knew her own name.

But he was certainly angry, which was fair since she probably shouldn't have used quite that tone with him. And maybe she was crazy, but she found it unbearably exciting. When she'd gone to live with her aunt and uncle, they had never taken much notice of her. They'd already had four other kids and hadn't wanted a sixth, especially one who wasn't theirs, so she'd been forgotten, ignored. Her middling marks at school and her middling performance at the outdoor activities they preferred had ensured her place as the most mediocre of their brood. Or perhaps the cuckoo in the nest was a more apt term, since the rest of their kids were blonde and tall, while she was dark-haired and short.

She'd once tried a bit of rebellion as a teenager by

sneaking a cigarette or two and going to a couple of parties, but even doing that hadn't earned her their attention. They hadn't even yelled at her. They'd shrugged their shoulders and ignored her, deeming her so unimportant they weren't even going to waste their anger.

But this man was wasting his anger on her, and God help her, but she liked it.

He was inches away, staring down at her, and she could smell his aftershave, spicy like sandalwood or frankincense, and it made her mouth go even drier than it already was. His body was large, hard, and powerful and he was hot; she could feel the heat of him radiating through his clothes.

His attention was fixed wholly on her as he put one hand on the wall beside her head. 'I don't want my date,' he said roughly, putting his other hand on the wall, caging her against it. 'I want you.'

Her heart thumped hard, deafening in her ears, electricity dancing like static over her skin. She looked into his eyes, the grey light in the centre of his iris darkening to charcoal around the edges. Fascinating eyes.

She wasn't afraid, even though he was crowding her. No, she was excited. Excited that she'd got to him, that she'd bothered him. Amazed that he found her beautiful. And thrilled beyond measure that he wanted her.

Because she wanted him too.

Nell took a sudden, shuddering breath and then, holding tight to her courage, she put out a hand and brushed her fingers along one of his high cheekbones. His skin was warm beneath her fingertips, whiskers making it slightly rough. 'Then what are you waiting for?' she said.

# CHAPTER THREE

ARISTOPHANES DIDN'T KNOW what was happening to him. He'd expected to come into her flat, dismiss the doctor, then perhaps order her to bed—rest was important—while he stayed up all night working. However, it was only once he'd arrived that he realised he hadn't brought anything to do his work on, and so he was looking at an entire evening of wasted time. An abhorrence that had made his already foul temper even fouler.

Dismissing the doctor hadn't been an issue, but then he'd heard the bathroom door open, so he'd gone into her tiny hallway only to find yet another aggravation: her standing there staring at him, wrapped up in the most ridiculous dressing gown he'd ever seen.

It was pink and fluffy, and she had a towel around her head, and she should not have looked so completely and utterly adorable. In addition, everything male in him knew she was naked beneath that dressing gown, and wanted to see if her skin was as pink as the robe and what would happen if he pulled at her towel and her hair tumbled down her back.

He wanted to know what would happen if he kissed her.

An absolutely unacceptable situation.

He'd been telling himself on the way over to her flat that it was only because he was worried about her, that was why he'd been drawn back to her. Nothing to do with the softness of her mouth, or the darkness of her eyes. Nothing to do with her delectable curves or the silkiness of her hair.

Physical attraction was nothing. It happened all the time. It wasn't special or singular.

It was the attraction of the mind that fascinated him, that drew him. He'd much rather have an interesting woman over a beautiful one any day of the week.

Yet right now, with her backed against the wall, looking up at him with darkened eyes, he didn't care about her mind. What he wanted was to rip aside all that fluffy pink and find the beautiful body beneath it. Touch it. Kiss it. Taste it.

Bury himself inside it.

It was the stupidest thing he'd ever felt and he was appalled by the baseness of his own desires. By how he seemed to have no control over them whatsoever.

He'd never, for example, become so angry with himself that he'd crowded a woman up against a door, or flung her own beauty back in her face. He'd never let himself care enough to even think about doing that.

Yet here he was, doing all of the above.

She should have been scared, since he was clearly behaving like a lunatic, yet instead she'd reached up and touched his face, her fingers soft against his cheek.

*What are you waiting for?* she'd said, the words hitting something deep inside him.

As if he'd been waiting indeed and now here she was, ready for him.

A preschool teacher... Not inherently bad, yet not on a par with Angelina, a professor at Harvard. Why had he left her for this woman? Why was his body insisting that Nell was what he wanted, when his head was positive it was Angelina?

'I don't know you,' he ground out, wanting her to understand. 'I don't do this with women I don't know.'

There was something soft in her eyes, something hot that sent fire all the way to his groin. She stroked his cheekbone lightly, as if he were hers to touch however and whenever she wished, and that didn't make any sense either. He didn't like people touching him when he wasn't in bed with them. He found it distracting.

Yet her touch... He wanted it. He *wanted* it.

'I don't do this with men I don't know,' she said in her husky voice. 'So, I suppose that makes us even.'

He should shove himself away, put some space between them. She'd hurt herself, for God's sake. What was he doing holding her against the door like this?

Yet he couldn't bring himself to move. His body wanted him to stay right here, where he could smell the soap and shampoo she'd used, something sweet and simple that made him ache for reasons he couldn't name. And she was so warm. He wanted to pull the tie of that ridiculous dressing gown, discover if she tasted as sweet as she smelled.

'Then why?' It was rapidly becoming difficult to think, which *never* happened to him, and he hated the feeling. Yet he seemed to be powerless against it. 'Why do you want me?' It was obvious to him why she'd want him—he was, after all, who he was. Yet he wanted to hear her say it. 'Why do you want *this*?'

Her silky red lashes lowered, fanning against her pink cheek. 'I… You're…' She paused, as if searching for the words, then her lashes lifted once more, her eyes wide and dark. 'When I was out, I dreamed of you, and when I woke up, you were holding my hand. And you're… beautiful. You're not like anyone I've ever met.'

He wanted to growl with satisfaction, an unbearably primitive response. Women wanted him, it was true. The lovers his assistants scheduled for him always, without exception, wanted him. He took it as read most of the time.

But the way Nell said it made him fierce and triumphant and feral.

It made him want to ravage her right here against the door.

He eased closer, so the pink fluffy edge of her dressing gown was brushing against his shirt. 'To be clear, I wanted sex tonight,' he said. 'So is that what you're offering?'

She flushed almost as pink as her robe, and yet she didn't look away. 'As it happens, I wanted sex tonight, too. But the man I was going to have it with ghosted me.'

Another thing he didn't understand. How could anyone have ghosted her?

'Why?' he demanded, suddenly enraged at the thought.

'He said I was too uptight.' She kept on staring at him, throwing the words at him like small hard stones. Challenging him, he thought. 'That I wasn't what he was looking for.'

For once, Aristophanes didn't think about the words that came out of his mouth and asked the question that had been taunting him all night. 'Was that why you weren't wearing any underwear? Was that for him?'

She flushed even deeper, making the darkness of her eyes even more apparent. 'Yes. But he never got to see under my dress because he ghosted me before I could show him.'

'Good,' he said fiercely. 'His loss is my gain. Why don't you show me, instead?'

She searched his face for one long moment, an emotion he couldn't name flickering in her gaze. Then her hand dropped from his cheekbone to the tie of her robe and she pulled it. The fluffy fabric of her robe slowly slid open.

And she was indeed as pink as her gown, her skin gloriously flushed from her shower, all freshly scrubbed and glowing and silky. Her breasts were as full as her curves had promised, and everywhere else she was gently rounded. She was biteable, lickable, and the sweet little thatch of auburn curls between her thighs…

God save him.

Satisfaction unfurled in him, lazy and hot, and he almost bared his teeth in yet another primitive growl. Yes, she wanted him. She wanted *him*.

She had her head half turned away, as if afraid to see his expression, so he reached for her chin and gripped it, turning her back to face him. 'Don't look away from me,' he ordered. 'You have nothing to be ashamed of.'

Instantly that little chin hardened in his grip. 'I'm not ashamed, I'm—'

'You're as beautiful as I said you were.' He wasn't sure why it was so important that she understand that. Perhaps it was only that the thought of a woman as gorgeous as this one being ghosted by some bastard who didn't realise what he had was insupportable. 'Shall I prove it to you?'

She took a breath, the pulse at the base of her throat racing frantically. Her eyes were dark as midnight and he couldn't stop himself from closing the gap between them, easing himself against her silky little body.

She shivered all over at the contact. 'Yes.' The word escaped on a breathless puff of sound, and he'd never heard anything so sweet. 'Please.'

He took one hand from beside her head then reached for one of her own, drawing it between them, looking into her face as he held her palm down over the front of his trousers, where he was so hard he ached.

Her eyes widened and her full mouth opened, her fingers giving a small convulsive squeeze that sent the breath from his lungs.

All rational thought had left his brain, all his higher thought processes non-functional. He was nothing but primitive hunger and base instinct now, and, for once in his life, he didn't care. So he didn't hide his reaction.

She should know what she did to him. Especially when he was going to do the same to her.

Holding her gaze, he lifted his other hand from the wall and gently laid it at the base of her throat, fingertips brushing the frantic beat of her pulse. She shivered, gasping softly, her head falling back slowly against the door, lashes lowering as he let his hand slide from her throat to the luscious curves of one breast. Her skin felt like silk, smooth and warm, the soft weight of her breast as his palm cupped it literally perfect.

She made a sound deep in her throat, her back arching as she pressed herself into his hand. Her nipple was hard and when he stroked his thumb slowly back and forth across it, teasing it, she made another of those passionate, wanton sounds.

Beautiful little woman.

Perfect little woman.

He bent his head and kissed her, taking one of those breathless moans into his mouth. She tasted exactly the way he'd thought she would, so sweet. No, she tasted even better, and now he was hungry. Starving.

He kissed her deeper, hotter, and she let him, arching against his hand as he teased the taut peak of her breast, and then kissing him back. She was unpractised, but that only added to the sweetness, and when she squeezed him again, slightly harder, the last trace of rational thought left his head.

There was only one thing he wanted now. Only one.

He wanted to be inside her and as quickly as possible.

\* \* \*

Nell had no idea how it had happened. How she'd got herself to this point, her dressing gown open, pressed up against a door as the world's most incredible man cupped her bare breast, turning her into a starving beast. But, however it had happened, she didn't care.

She should be resting and nursing her head, yet all that pain had vanished, lost under the onslaught of the most overwhelming tide of pleasure. She'd never dreamed her body would be capable of this, and yet she couldn't deny what she felt now. It was glorious.

Aristophanes Katsaros was better than any drug.

His hand gently stroking her, the press of his muscular body. The heat of him. The hard length of his shaft pressing against the material of his trousers and into her palm. A big man in every way.

She'd lost her virginity to her first boyfriend in her last year of high school. It had been a very disappointing and embarrassing ten minutes in the back of his car and she hadn't been in any hurry to repeat the experience. But then she'd met Clayton and…

Well. She and Clayton had never got this far, and she'd told herself it was because she'd wanted to wait, but now she knew that was a lie. She'd never wanted to wait. She'd never wanted Clayton at all. Not as she wanted this man, this stranger who'd rescued her unconscious from a rainy street. Who'd held her hand and cared enough about her to make sure she was okay.

Who'd made her feel more wanted than anyone else ever had in her entire life.

Perhaps that was why she'd found the courage to pull the tie on her dressing gown, baring herself to him. That and the look in his eyes. *Why don't you show me, instead?* he'd ordered and all she'd been able to think about was yes, yes, she wanted to show him. She wanted him to see her.

Her courage had left her for a second the moment her gown had fallen open, but then he'd taken her chin in his hand and turned her back to face him, his silvery gaze electric, blazing with fire. There had been no doubt that he'd liked what he saw and he'd wanted her to know that too.

Now she couldn't imagine anything she wanted more than to strip away the confining material of her dressing gown. Pull open his shirt, touch his skin. Be naked with him. They'd both been intending to have sex so why not? They could have it now, right here, she didn't care. She'd have him any way he wanted it.

Nell moaned into his mouth as his hand slid from her breast down over her stomach, fingertips grazing the curls between her thighs. 'Yes,' she breathed, hardly aware she'd even spoken. 'Oh, yes, please…'

He gave another of those deep, sexy growls and then his fingertips were sliding over the slick, sensitive skin of her sex, exploring, stroking, teasing. She shuddered and, without thought, reached for the button of his fly, desperate to touch him as he was touching her. But then he growled again, pulling away, and before she could process what was going on, he'd dropped to his knees in front of her.

She barely had time to gasp before his hands gripped her hips, pinning her hard against the door, and his mouth was on her stomach, licking a slow, lazy path down to where she was hot and wet, and so needy she thought she'd die.

He held her against the wood, nuzzling against her, licking, exploring, tasting. Then his tongue found the most sensitive part of her and flicked over it, making her shudder and shake. Her hands were buried in his hair, the thick black strands silky against her fingers, and she gripped him tight, unable to hold in the sounds he brought from her.

No one had ever touched her like this, tasted her like this.

No one had ever made her the sole focus of their attention.

No one had ever made her feel as if she was being slowly and thoroughly worshipped, as if they couldn't get enough of her.

No one had ever made her feel as if she might die from pleasure.

Her eyes drifted closed, colours swirling behind her closed lids as everything inside her drew tight, as if she were an arrow about to be launched into the sky.

'That's it,' she heard him murmur, his breath against her skin as she trembled. 'Scream for me, woman. Scream, so I can hear it.'

Then he did something with his tongue and she did

scream, pleasure unleashing in a wild storm through her body, her cries echoing in the small space of the hallway as the orgasm took her.

She was still panting, wondering how on earth she was standing upright, when his hands slid beneath her thighs and she was lifted against the door as if she weighed nothing. He pinned her there with his body, holding her pressed to the wood effortlessly, and his hand was back between her thighs, touching her, stroking her back into trembling hunger once again. Then he pulled open his fly, spread her delicately with his fingers before pushing into her slowly, so very slowly.

His silver gaze didn't leave hers, pinning her as surely as his body, holding her mesmerised as she felt her body open for him, stretching to take him. She groaned, nothing but the feel of him inside her, a heavy, aching fullness that made her want to pant and claw at his back.

'You are perfect.' His voice was raw, guttural, and he bent, his teeth grazing the tender skin of her shoulder, making her shiver in delight. 'Absolutely perfect.'

She had never felt perfect. She'd always felt as if there was something missing, something that made her less interesting, less intriguing, less worthy almost, than her cousins. They were mystified by her, and so were her aunt and uncle. Sometimes she felt as if they didn't know what to do with her and—worse—weren't interested in finding out, so they just left her to her own devices.

Now, even though her towel had fallen from her head and her wet hair was draped like seaweed across her shoulders, and her dressing gown was half off, she didn't feel uninteresting or unworthy. She didn't feel as if she was missing something.

She felt beautiful. As if she really was as perfect as he'd told her she was.

Nell squeezed her legs around his waist, pulled his shirt half open and slid her hands inside it, feeling the hot velvet of his skin. He was all hard muscle, the crisp brush of hair, and he smelled spicy and musky and male, and she was desperate for him.

He was perfect too.

Then he began to move and everything slid away. Her embarrassment and shame at Clayton's no-show. Her anger at Aristophanes' overbearing manner. Her self-consciousness and fear that this would end the way so many of her relationships with people had ended, with her not being enough for anyone… They all vanished. There was no room for them, not when the pleasure inside her was growing and filling every space.

A part of herself she'd never realised she had, a more primal part, began to take over. It was hungry and passionate, with no inhibitions. It only wanted more of the pleasure he was giving her, making her sink her nails into his back and moan as he moved deeper, harder.

But while she might have lost all sense, he apparently hadn't, because she felt him slide one of his hands behind her head, cupping the base of her skull in his large, warm palm, projecting her injury as he moved inside her.

For a second Nell loved him for that. Then the knife edge of pleasure grew sharper, and she felt again the tightness gather, the bow being drawn back, ready to launch her into the sky. He shifted, changing his angle, the friction so perfect it brought tears to her eyes, and then the tightness inside her was released and she was flying, soaring into the sky in a wild, glorious rush. Dimly she heard him say her name in a low, guttural roar before he too joined her in the sky.

Time passed as she floated slowly back down to earth, both of them still leaning against her bedroom door locked together as if nothing could tear them apart, their breathing slowly easing.

This moment, too, was perfect, and she didn't want to move. Yet then she felt him shift his grip on her, lowering her to the floor, cold air moving over her heated skin as he pulled away. His hands gently pulled her robe closed, wrapping her up, and it hit her suddenly that he was preparing to leave.

Nell didn't think. Operating entirely on instinct, she reached out and grabbed his hand, holding on. 'Don't go,' she said and if it came out sounding a little more desperate than she wanted it to, she didn't care.

He went still, his gaze full of storm clouds. 'I'm not. I have to stay with you for twenty-four hours, remember?'

'That's not what I meant.' She took a little breath. 'I meant stay with me.'

His beautiful face was unreadable, yet there was lightning in his eyes as he looked at her. 'There can be nothing more than this, Nell,' he said after a long moment. 'Only a night. We can never see each other again after that, understood?'

There was a second where she wanted to know why, but then dismissed the thought. It didn't matter why. The only thing that mattered was that he was here and he wanted her, and that once wasn't enough for either of them.

'Understood,' she said hoarsely.

The quality of his attention changed then, sharpening, focusing on her, studying her as if she was a complex problem he was desperate to solve. 'How are you feeling?'

She felt something inside her release then, in a silent exhale. 'Pretty good. Though... I could always feel better.'

His gaze became pure silver. 'The doctor is gone, but perhaps you need my help?'

'I do,' she agreed, her heartbeat already ramping up.

His fingers tightened around hers. 'Then come here, woman. Show me where it hurts and I'll kiss it better.'

# CHAPTER FOUR

THE ELEVATOR DOORS opened and Aristophanes stepped inside. He'd just finished up a meeting in his New York office in downtown Manhattan, and, according to his schedule, he had half an hour to get uptown to meet Claire, an astrophysicist who'd been working with CERN, and whom he'd been trying to match schedules with for the past week.

Or at least, his secretaries had been trying to match schedules. This was their third attempt to find an evening that suited both him and Claire, and, if this fell through, Aristophanes was thinking he might not bother at all. They'd met at a fundraiser and she'd been interesting, and there had been enough chemistry between them that he'd told her that if she'd wanted a liaison, he'd be happy to oblige. She had and so his secretarial team had swung into action.

Yet he was feeling restless and off kilter, and strangely enervated at the thought of sex with Claire. Almost as if he didn't want her, which would be the fourth time this month that he hadn't wanted a woman. It had been the same the month before that too.

If he really thought about it, he'd felt the same since he'd had that one night in Melbourne three months earlier, with the perfect little preschool teacher.

He didn't like to think about that night. He didn't like to think about what they'd done in her small bedroom in her small, cluttered flat. They hadn't talked. They hadn't had any kind of conversation at all; they'd let their bodies talk instead, their conversation wild and passionate, without boundaries or limits. They'd done everything and anything, and, for once in his life, his brain had gone quiet and still. Silenced by raw hunger and need.

He'd left her fast asleep the next morning, organising his doctor to give her a final check-up. Then he'd pushed her to the back of his mind as far as she would go. As far away from his consciousness as possible.

He'd been busy these past few months, flying between his offices in various countries, never staying too long anywhere, which was his preference. He'd paid a visit to Cesare Donati, a good friend—possibly his only friend—whom he'd known for years, and who was the owner of one of Italy's largest private banks. Cesare had recently married a lovely Englishwoman called Lark, and had spent Aristophanes' visit proudly showing off his little daughter, Maya, whom Aristophanes, who'd never had anything to do with children, found rather more interesting than he'd expected. The little girl had even lifted her arms to him, wanting to be picked up, so he had, then had felt oddly at a loss as to what to do next.

Maya had looked at him with big blue eyes, babbling on about something, and he, who knew many different languages and a lot of them fluently, hadn't understood a word. He'd found himself staring at her in stunned silence, a nagging sensation in his chest that didn't make any sense. The child was a mystery, and he loved a good mystery, a good, complicated puzzle, yet there was another part of him that wanted to put her down and get as far away from her as he could.

Having children of his own had never occurred to him and if he'd ever thought deeply about it, he would have said he didn't want them. Children could not operate on his schedule, for a start, and he didn't have enough time for them even if they could. They demanded too much, and he was a man who demanded of others. He did not meet *their* demands.

Still, he couldn't deny that having Maya and Lark had changed Cesare's life and for the better. His friend had found happiness, it was clear, and Aristophanes was pleased for him.

But family life was not and could not be for him.

He was a man of the mind, of the intellect, and it was cerebral topics that interested him, not home and hearth.

Aristophanes hit the button for the first floor and the elevator moved smoothly into life, descending through the sleek steel and glass skyscraper that housed the New York office of Katsaros International, and down into the vast, glass-ceilinged hall that was the foyer.

As Aristophanes stepped out, a gentle commotion at the imposing front desk caught his attention. A woman was standing on her tiptoes, her hands on the edges of the desk as she tried to make herself taller, leaning into it and saying something urgently to Karina, who managed the front desk.

A small woman. Wearing a voluminous black coat against the early spring New York weather, the shoulders of which were wet with rain. As was her auburn hair, hanging down her back in a thick braid.

Karina was shaking her head with emphasis, then she glanced over to the security guards near the entrance and gestured to them.

Aristophanes should have continued on. He should have walked right past the little woman making a fuss at his front desk. Many people wanted entrance to his building and many people were turned away. Certainly, if it was him they wanted to see then they were out of luck. His schedule was full for the next month.

So he wasn't sure why he stopped dead in his tracks, his gaze fixed on the woman at the desk. There was something familiar about her. Something familiar about the thick auburn hair hanging down her back. It reminded him of that night in Melbourne, of Nell, his Burne-Jones angel with her thick and silky hair that he'd gathered in his fist as he'd driven inside her from behind, making her bed shake...

The woman turned her head slightly and an arrow of desire so intense it stopped his breath pierced him.

It *was* her.

Nell.

She hadn't seen him, still talking urgently to Karina, who was now shaking her head as a couple of security

guards came over. Clearly they were on the point of es-
corting Nell from the building.

His thoughts seemed to stop in their tracks, over-
whelmed utterly by the reality of her, and then, with
the same abruptness, they began to move again and this
time at lightning speed.

She was here. In New York. In his building. Which
must mean she wanted to see him. Why? He'd told her
it could only be one night and she'd agreed. He'd left her
sleeping and she'd been as good as her word. He hadn't
heard from her since.

Something must have changed, something urgent
enough that she'd come to see him herself. Something
important enough that it required a face-to-face meeting and out of the blue.

For a second his brain furiously sorted through all
the possibilities until there was only one left. One that
made him go icy with shock.

He'd thought they'd been careful with protection that
night. Every time, he'd used a condom. Also, she'd told
him she'd been on the pill in preparation for giving herself to that pathetic, ungrateful boyfriend of hers.

But…now he thought about it, he couldn't remember using protection that first time up against her bedroom door. He'd been so hungry for her, so desperate,
so motivated by his own base instinct, he hadn't even
thought about it.

There was a failure rate for the pill. It was slim, but
it was there, and it only took once…

The shock penetrated the whole way through his body

and then something else seemed to ignite in his chest. Smouldering, leaping into flame, burning hot…

She *must* be pregnant. That was why she was there, that was the only reason he could think of, and it would certainly explain the urgency with which she was talking. And how she gripped onto the front desk with her fingers as one of his security guards took her arm, trying to urge her away, then pulling…

'Stop,' Aristophanes said coldly, his voice echoing in the vaulted spaces of the foyer.

Everyone standing at the front desk froze, then turned.

And the fierce burning in his chest shifted and changed as Nell Underwood's dark eyes met his then widened, her creamy skin flushing with colour. His body hardened almost instantly, his brain no help at all as images of their night together began playing in his head.

Ruthlessly, he shoved them aside, ignored the demands of his body, and strode over to where Nell was standing, staring at him like a deer in the headlights of a car. 'Leave this to me,' he ordered to the security guards and Karina, who all obediently went back to their posts as if nothing had happened. Then he looked down into Nell's beautiful face. 'You,' he said. 'You're coming with me.'

It wasn't a question and he didn't give her a chance to protest. He took her arm in an unbreakable grip and urged her over to the elevators.

'I'm coming, I'm coming,' she said irritably, though she didn't resist him. 'You don't need to manhandle me. I was actually here to see you.'

'I thought as much.' He hit the button for his private elevator and, though every base instinct in his body was screaming at him to keep hold of her, he released his grip on her arm. 'You didn't have an appointment.'

The doors opened smoothly and he ushered her inside. As they shut, he pressed the button for his office and the elevator began to rise.

'No, I didn't.' She'd taken a few steps away from him, as if she wanted to put some distance between them. It grated on his nerves for reasons he couldn't have explained. Her hands moved restlessly, adjusting her coat and smoothing her damp hair. 'That woman at the front desk told me it was impossible to see you,' she said, her familiar voice clear as a bell. 'That you were booked up for an entire month, and even if there was a space in your schedule, you wouldn't be able to see me, because you were far too important.'

'I am,' he said without irony, because it was no less than the truth. 'However, I find I have some time now.' He didn't, of course. Claire was waiting for him. Yet Claire seemed to be the least important thing to him in this moment.

Nell's dark gaze was wary, but that little chin of hers was stubborn. He remembered taking it in his fingers, remembered how warm her skin had been and how silky it had felt. 'Why now?' she asked.

'Because you are here.' He met her gaze head-on. 'I thought I told you that you weren't to contact me again.'

'You did.' She made another nervous adjustment to her coat. 'And believe me, I wouldn't have done so.

But…' A breath escaped her and she swallowed. 'I need to tell you something.'

He could smell her scent, sweet and tantalising, and the fire in his chest seemed to burn brighter, hotter. He was going to be so late for Claire, but, now that he was here in this elevator with Nell, he couldn't think of anything he wanted less than to leave and find a different woman. A woman who wasn't Nell.

*Remember why she's here.*

Ah, yes. There was that.

'Yes,' Aristophanes said. 'You're here to tell me you're pregnant.'

Nell had no idea how he'd guessed. She was too busy trying to get some air into her lungs, an impossible task when Aristophanes seemed to take up every square inch of the extremely small space of the elevator. And not only with his tall, muscular body, but also with the electrical charge of his magnetic presence.

He was so very intense.

She hadn't forgotten how beautiful he was, but she *had* forgotten how physically devastating he was in the flesh. She could almost feel her body readying itself for him, which was disconcerting in the extreme, especially since it had been three months since she'd last seen him. Apparently, though, it didn't matter how long it had been. She still wanted him with the same hunger as she had back then.

The past six weeks had been such a roller coaster. First there had been the shock of discovering she was pregnant and then a barrage of appointments to make sure everything was looking as it should. Then there had been the nausea and exhaustion of early pregnancy, as well as the uncertainty of what she was going to do about the baby.

That she was going to keep it had never been in doubt—she'd always wanted children and, despite the timing being horrendous, she desperately wanted to keep this one. However, she felt very strongly that a child should have two parents. She'd lost hers so early and it was a constant grief to her, and she couldn't imagine her own child not having them.

It made letting Aristophanes know he was going to be a father imperative. She'd decided to wait until after the twelve-week mark just to be sure, but after emails, phone calls and requests to speak with him had all fallen through, she'd eventually booked a ticket to New York since that was where he apparently was for the next month. She hadn't had much in the way of savings, but it had been enough for a flight and some cheap accommodation, which wasn't very cheap because it was New York.

She'd debated about how to tell him, because he'd been very clear he didn't want to see her again and likely wouldn't welcome the news he was going to be a father. But that was too bad. She didn't want his money; she wanted only his presence in their child's life. That was all.

So all the way on that long, interminable flight from Melbourne to JFK, she'd gone over and over in her head what she was going to say to him. How she was going to tell him. Then, in the end, he'd taken the words straight out of her mouth.

The pedantic fool.

She stood in her damp coat, in the too-small space of the elevator, staring into his silver eyes. Conscious once again of his physical beauty. He was even taller than she remembered, his magnificent physique clad in what had to be a handmade suit of dark grey wool that seemed to highlight every inch of his broad shoulders and wide chest. His pristine black shirt was offset with a silver silk tie the exact colour of his eyes, and she wished she'd chosen something better to wear than the cheap rust-red dress she'd bought at a chain store because it was stretchy and would go over the little bump that was beginning to show.

Sadly, it was too late for that. She hadn't had the money to buy anything decent anyway, not after the extortionate flight had been paid for.

She shivered as his intense silver gaze scanned her from the top of her damp head to the wet black leather of her pumps, and back up again. The elevator seemed to get smaller and smaller, the air in it thicker and thicker.

'Thanks for completely ruining my announcement,' she said, unable to hide her irritation. She hadn't been in his presence more than a minute and already he was getting under her skin. How he managed to do that, she couldn't fathom.

The first few weeks after their night together, she'd pushed him firmly to the back of her mind, because he'd said they'd never see each other again, and she'd agreed. Then after she'd discovered she was pregnant, the night they'd spent together had flooded back into her consciousness and had been taunting her ever since.

She'd thought she wouldn't want him again. She'd thought that one night was enough. Yet here she was, cold and jet-lagged and irritable, and all she could think about was putting her hands on his broad chest and pulling the buttons of his shirt open, pressing her mouth to his skin, tasting him…

Aristophanes tilted his head, the silver in his eyes glittering brighter as his gaze roved hungrily over her. And yes, it was hungry. The three months since she'd last seen him might as well not have existed. He might have been standing once again in the hallway of her small flat, staring at her as though he wanted to eat her alive.

Nell swallowed, her irritation turning into something more intense yet no less unsettling, her heartbeat thumping loudly in her ears.

The tension filling the elevator car felt almost unbearable.

'Mr Katsaros,' she began determinedly.

Abruptly and without a word, he dropped the briefcase he was carrying and took two steps towards her, forcing her back against the rail that ran around the interior of the elevator at waist height.

The look in his eyes burned, making an intense burst of wild excitement flood through her in response, an excitement she'd only ever felt once before: in his arms.

Oh, Lord, he wanted her and badly.

Slowly and with intent, he put one hand on the rail next to her, then the other hand, caging her against it the way he'd caged her against the door back in her Melbourne flat. And now, as then, she was acutely conscious of his warmth, of the musky spice of his aftershave.

It was intoxicating. She hadn't realised how cold she'd been until he was here.

He didn't move, only stared at her, his gaze searching her face as if looking for something. She couldn't get enough air, the only sound her heartbeat thumping crazily in her ears.

'Don't,' she breathed shakily, even though he hadn't said anything or moved another inch. She only knew if he did, she'd be lost, and she didn't want to be lost, not with this baby literally between them. Also, they needed to talk, not do...*this*.

'Don't?' he echoed, a thread of heat running through his deep, dark voice like fire in a coal seam. 'Don't what?'

Her breathing was getting faster and faster, the physical electricity he was throwing off making it difficult to think. He was standing so close, the gap between them mere inches.

'This,' she breathed, her voice husky. 'Don't do... this.'

Again, he didn't move closer, only lifted a hand and took her chin in his large, warm fingers, tilting her head back to look at him. His gaze burned so brightly she couldn't look away.

'Three months,' he murmured, his attention dropping to her mouth and then back up again. 'That's how long it's been since I've had a woman. And that's all your fault.'

Something inside her dropped away.

He hadn't slept with anyone in three months? Was he serious? There really had been no one since her?

'M-my fault?' she said unsteadily.

'Yes, yours.' His thumb stroked over her bottom lip, making her tremble. 'Every woman I have tried to spend time with hasn't interested me, and I thought it was because I've been working too hard. I thought it was because I was tired.' He paused, a flame in his eyes. 'Then you suddenly appear in my goddamn building, and now all I can think about is how to get you naked as quickly as humanly possible.'

The warmth of his touch was radiating through her entire body, chasing away the cold and the irritation, and somehow the jet lag too. She felt like a sunflower starved of light, turning towards the sun.

*You didn't come here for sex, remember? You came here to talk.*

That was true, but she'd felt nothing but uncertain for weeks and weeks. She'd been physically sick and anxious, and afraid of what would happen with the baby, what her life would look like after it was born. And now he was here and he wanted her with the same fierceness as he'd wanted her three months earlier. He'd made her feel so good, so beautiful and sexy, and desirable, and she wanted more of that; she couldn't deny it.

So why couldn't she have it? Have one more good experience before reality hit. A few more moments of pleasure, before her child arrived and took over her world.

He was still a stranger to her as much as he had been that night, but she didn't care. She hadn't realised how badly she'd been craving his touch until now.

'I...' She couldn't stop looking at his mouth, remembering how it had felt on her skin. Remembering its softness and the dark taste of him. 'I...don't think this is a good idea.'

'I disagree.' His head dipped, his mouth inches from hers. 'Did you know I was on my way to see someone else tonight when you turned up?'

'No.' The word escaped her on a sigh, the only thing of any importance his mouth so close to hers. 'I didn't know.'

'Woman, this is the second time you've ruined my evening plans.'

Nell wanted him to kiss her more than she'd wanted anything in her entire life. 'Perhaps it's fate,' she breathed.

'I don't care what it is.' His voice had deepened into that low growl that stroked over her skin like a hand. 'But if you don't want to have sex in this elevator, I suggest you tell me now.'

It was the raw note in the words that got her. The desperation that turned her inside out. She hadn't been able to resist his hunger for her all those months ago and she couldn't resist it now. She lifted her hands, took his face between them and pulled his mouth down on hers.

The kiss was blinding, a fire that once ignited couldn't be put out and it blazed high.

He made a rough sound in the back of his throat and abruptly his hands were on her hips, lifting her effortlessly onto the rail at her back. Then he glanced down, touching the little bump of her stomach almost in greeting, before pushing up her dress and spreading her knees wide so he could stand between them.

She gasped as he caressed the outside of her thighs then shuddered as his fingers slid inward, seeking more sensitive parts of her. A harsh sound of male satisfaction broke from him as he pulled aside her underwear and stroked over the slick heat of her sex, discovering how wet she was already for him.

She liked that sound. It thrilled her, as did the pleasure flooding through her, saturating every cell, making her arch back against the wall, glorying in his touch.

He bent his head then and kissed her again, devouring her utterly as his fingers teased and caressed her slick flesh, making her shift and move against his hand, desperate for more.

'Tell me where you want me,' he demanded, low and rough against her mouth. 'Tell me exactly.'

Nell was trembling, remembering how he'd demanded similar things from her that night they'd spent together and how she'd given them to him. Every single thing.

She wanted to do the same now.

'I want you inside me,' she said huskily, unable to hide the desperation in her voice.

He lifted his head, silver eyes burning. 'Now? Here?'

'Yes,' she whispered. 'Now. Here. Please...'

He didn't wait.

Almost in one movement, he turned, hit the stop button on the elevator, then turned back to her, tearing open his trousers and freeing himself. Then he gripped her hips and pushed hard and deep inside her, making her groan at the delicious burn and stretch of him.

It was too good. Too perfect. He made all her jet lag and cold and exhaustion just disappear and she didn't know how, but she didn't question it. She felt better than she had for months and she wanted more.

He'd paused, deep inside her, and she didn't look away as he stared at her, letting him know how good he was making her feel without words. Then she lifted her hand and touched his face, her fingers trembling, mesmerised by the feel of his skin. Warm and smooth, and yet some parts of it rough with whiskers.

He'd been beautiful back in Melbourne and he was still beautiful now.

He began to move, a slow rhythm that made her twist and arch against him, the fever beginning to build inside her until she had no idea where she was or even who she was. She only knew the pleasure growing wider, deeper, vaster than space.

'You,' she whispered to him, falling headlong into the melted silver of his eyes. 'What are you doing to me?'

'Only what you're doing to me.' He took her mouth again in a raw, demanding kiss that sent every last remaining thought from her head.

There was nothing after that. Nothing except the bonfire of pleasure they built between them, the flames leaping high. Then a final blaze into the sky with a wild rush of sparks before falling back, leaving both of them nothing but glowing embers.

She rested her forehead against his shoulder, panting as her heartbeat began to slow, the aftershocks still rocking her. He didn't move, a warm wall of hard muscle for her to rest against, and so she did.

She didn't want to think about what would happen next.

She didn't want to think at all.

She'd just had sex with the father of her child within minutes of meeting him for the second time. And she had no idea at all what she was going to do with that.

# CHAPTER FIVE

ARISTOPHANES STARED AT the slightly reflective steel wall at Nell's back, thanking God he couldn't see his own reflection. Because he was pretty sure he'd find himself looking into the eyes of a complete fool.

A fool who'd thrown both his intellect and self-control straight out of the window in favour of parts located below his belt.

He was appalled at himself. Again.

What magic did this woman possess that she made him lose his head every time he saw her? The smallness of the elevator hadn't helped, it was true, making it impossible to put distance between them. And all he'd been conscious of was the scent of her, so sweet and feminine, and that yet again she was wearing a dress that outlined every luscious curve of her body, including the little bump of her stomach where his child lay.

A heated, raw feeling had flooded through him then, primitive and possessive, that had made him want to back her against the wall and claim her, make her his in every way.

He'd fought the urge, battled it hard, yet he hadn't

been able to drag his gaze from hers. Her dark eyes had been velvet soft and he'd seen them heat in response to him, getting even hotter the longer they stared at each other. Then the tension had pulled tighter and tighter until he'd known he had to take some kind of action, otherwise he'd go mad.

He shouldn't have backed her up against the wall, but he had. And then she'd reached for him, drawing his mouth down on hers and…he'd lost himself. Lost himself as completely and utterly as he had that night with her three months earlier.

Perhaps he should have done what he'd intended to do tonight, sent Nell away and gone to see Claire. But… he couldn't even remember Claire's face or the sound of her voice, not with Nell slumped against him, her forehead resting against his shoulder, her face pressed to the cotton of her shirt, the warmth of her breath soaking through the fabric and into him…

*She's pregnant with your child. If you claim her, you could have her close whenever you needed her. You wouldn't have to do all that matching schedules nonsense…*

Aristophanes went very still as the thought struck him and echoed.

What if he could have her—have this—any time he wanted? He'd still have to schedule time with her, but it would be much more efficient to schedule it with a woman he knew he wanted and who would satisfy his bodily needs.

As for his child, he already knew that he wouldn't

abandon it. He'd never do to his own son or daughter what his mother had done to him. He was a better man than that.

Of course, he had no idea how to be a father, but surely it couldn't be too hard. Cesare had managed it and his little girl seemed to be a happy, normal child despite having him for a father. That might have been down to Lark, Cesare's wife, but that was why a child had two parents. He'd only ever had one since he'd never known who his father was and he felt no urge to find out. Any man who abandoned his child was as bad as his mother, in Aristophanes' opinion.

He wasn't sure if Nell was here for child support or something else but, given their physical chemistry, he'd already decided what he was going to do. She might not be open to it, but he was confident he could convince her. He could be persuasive when he wanted to be.

Time was passing, the minutes ticking by, and now was not the time to be standing here. They needed to talk. Also, he needed to tell the secretaries who managed his diary to arrange an appropriate apology gift for Claire, since he wouldn't be meeting her after all. It was also likely that they were going to have to rearrange his schedule to accommodate…other things. A child, for one. Possibly a woman for another.

Now, though, Nell had to be dealt with, so he eased himself away from her, obtaining yet more satisfaction from the slight sound of protest she made at his retreat.

'We need to talk,' he murmured as he helped her down from the rail so she was standing, unable to resist tracing the curve of her stomach where his child lay, a fleeting, possessive touch before he rearranged her clothes and dealt with his own. 'I have made some decisions.' He turned to the elevator doors, hitting the button once again.

The elevator shuddered into life and resumed its climb to his office.

'What decisions?' she asked, her clear voice pleasantly husky.

The sound of it shivered over his skin, the knowledge that she sounded like that because of the orgasm he'd given her making him hard all over again.

Yes, this was clearly something he was going to have to deal with. His physical response to her either needed to be nipped in the bud or indulged to its fullest extent until he didn't feel it any more.

Since she was pregnant and he would not abandon his child, indulging it seemed to be the best course of action.

He turned and looked down at her.

She was in the process of smoothing down the dress she wore, the fabric clinging deliciously to her curves, and he couldn't help raking his gaze hungrily down her body. If he kept her for a time, he could dress her in expensive gowns, of the finest material, that he could then tear off. Or maybe he would simply cover her naked body in jewels. He had more money than he knew what to do with… Why not?

Her cheeks were flushed and as he stared at her, she went an even deeper shade of rose.

'Decisions about you,' he said as the elevator arrived at his floor and chimed. 'About the child.'

She blinked, clearly still coming back down to earth. 'What about me and the child?'

The doors opened then so he turned back, taking her hand and stepping out directly into his vast office.

It occupied one corner of the top floor of his sky-scraper, a huge, open-plan space with little islands of furniture dotted here and there. A desk positioned near the acres of floor-to-ceiling windows with a chair on the other side of it. Then across the pale carpet stood a meeting table surrounded by chairs. Near one of the other windows was a sectional couch of bone-coloured leather. A huge whiteboard covered in complicated maths equations stood by itself in the centre of the space.

The whiteboard and the desk were the main things he used, the space between the other bits and pieces of furniture where he paced up and down while he ran projections and equations in his head.

She came with him as he went over to his desk, her hand in his small and warm, and didn't resist as he guided her to the chair that stood in front of it.

'Sit,' he murmured.

He didn't want to release her, but he forced his fingers to uncurl from hers, helping her into the chair, even though she didn't need him to. It was difficult to keep from touching her, a light hand on the small of her back, a passing brush to her elbow.

She glanced up at him as she settled, dark eyes burning. Some of her hair had escaped its braid and was curling around her face, her cheeks still stained the prettiest shade of pink. And again he felt the same burst of satisfaction as he had when his fingers had quested between her thighs and found her warm and wet and ready for him.

He'd put that flush in her cheeks. He'd put that dark passion in her eyes.

It was primitive, that satisfaction, and he should be wary of it. Should be forcing it aside, along with all those other bothersome biological responses.

It wasn't that he denied his body—it was, after all, the vessel that contained his mind and so he looked after it, made sure it stayed in optimal condition. But he resented anything that distracted his intellect, and most especially when he was working.

*A child is certainly going to distract your intellect.*

The thought crept through him, making every muscle get tight, a burning sensation in his chest. No, a child would not distract him. He wouldn't let it. He'd keep both the child and the woman close, keep them near so he could keep any such distractions to a minimum.

Forcing his recalcitrant feelings back into the box he kept them in, Aristophanes strode around the side of the desk then sat down in the vast black leather chair behind it.

'So,' he said. 'These decisions. The child is mine, correct?'

Nell's eyes widened slightly in surprise then narrowed, her full mouth compressing. 'Of course the child is yours. I haven't been with anyone else since you.'

For a moment a weighted silence hung between them and he found himself staring into those velvety eyes of hers, the memories of that night filling the vast space of his office with heat and desperation, and the most intense physical pleasure. It was clear she was sharing in those memories, too, because her gaze darkened even further, turning smoky, the tightness leaving her lovely mouth, her lips parting just a touch.

They'd had sex mere moments before and yet he could feel his desire rising yet again, heating the blood in his veins and making him hard. If he let this silence go on too much longer, he wasn't going to be able to stay in his chair. He was going to lunge across the desk and grab her, drag her into his lap like a lion with an antelope.

She took a soft breath. 'Mr Katsaros—'

'I have many houses scattered across the globe,' he said abruptly, forcing the desire away, trying to get some control back. 'You choose which one you prefer to bring our child up in.'

Nell blinked. 'Excuse me?'

'You will live with the child in one of my houses. I don't care which it is.'

'I… I don't—'

'If finances are a problem, I will take care of it.' He found himself gripping the arms of his chair as if that were the only thing stopping him from reaching for her. 'You and the child will want for nothing.'

The smoky look had vanished from her eyes and they sharpened. 'You…want me to live with you?'

'No, not with me.' He wasn't used to having to explain

himself. He'd always thought it a waste of precious time, and he resented having to do so now. It was this need, though, that was the problem. This desire wrapping its hands around his throat and squeezing him, choking him, making it difficult to think. He never found it difficult to think. 'I do not live anywhere in particular. You will have one of my houses and the child will be raised there.'

The desire had vanished utterly from her gaze, giving way to shock. 'You're joking,' she said. 'I mean, seriously?'

Annoyance started to bite. At himself and the desire that wouldn't seem to leave him alone, that he couldn't control. At her and her beauty, and the way his body had fixated on her for some reason. At how she clouded his mind and made it difficult to think.

His mind had been his sanctuary, the perfect escape from the drudgery of living ever since he'd been a child. An escape from loneliness, from anger, from longing. A private world where he was the master. That mastery now extended into the real world and he would allow no one to compromise it, still less one little preschool teacher from Melbourne, no matter how lovely she was.

'No,' he said flatly. 'I am not. The child is mine, my heir. He or she will also need a mother, therefore your presence will be required.' He paused, his fingers clenched around the arms of his chair. 'Your presence will also be required in my bed.' His jaw felt tight, a muscle leaping there. It felt as if he were trying to hold back the tide. 'And that, Miss Underwood, is non-ne-gotiable. Do you understand?'

Nell stared at the man sitting across the acres of dark oak.

He sat like a king, the vast black leather chair his throne, his gaze boring into hers. It burned that gaze, nothing but molten silver, making her feel hot all over.

She'd thought that maybe those feverish frantic moments in the elevator would have blunted the edge of her own desire, but they hadn't. If anything they had only intensified it, made her hungry for more. It hadn't been water on a fire but gasoline, and now she felt as if he'd burned away some vital part of her, a layer that had been protecting her, leaving her vulnerable and raw and, yes, still desperate for him.

Perhaps it was a combination of pregnancy hormones and shock. Or maybe it was just him. Him and the all-consuming way he looked at her, as if he was as hungry for her as she was for him.

Still. Even after three months had passed.

God, she couldn't look away.

Tension radiated from him, a muscle leaping in the side of his strong jaw, his hands gripping the arms of his chair as if he was afraid what he might do if he let go.

*You did that to him. That was all you.*

He wanted her and she'd loved that hunger of his. She hadn't had to do a thing. She'd just been herself and now she had this powerful man, this billionaire who owned the towering skyscraper she was sitting in, ravenous for her.

It was intoxicating, a welcome respite from the months of uncertainty and fear and constant exhaustion, and she wanted more of it. She hadn't tested the boundaries of her effect on him back in Melbourne that night, not when they'd been too busy with their basic hunger for each other, but now she wanted to. She wanted to test her power.

*Get it together. He's basically demanding you sleep with him again, remember?*

Nell took a sudden breath. What had he said? That he wanted her and the baby to live in one of his houses, and she would be in his bed. And that was non-negotiable.

Awareness flooded back in, cold as ice, washing away the heat and the pulse of desire.

She struggled to shake off the force of his intense gaze. 'That's…not why I came here,' she said, trying to get rid of the husk in her voice. 'I don't want your money.'

He didn't move, his beautiful face set in hard lines. 'Then why did you come?'

'You know why. I told you.'

'The baby, yes. But that could have been a phone call. What else did you want?'

'I didn't have your number and no one would give it to me, and I thought…this was a conversation we should have face to face.' Her hands twisted in her lap, the adrenaline coursing through her making her feel restless and antsy. 'Our baby needs a father and I wanted to give you the chance to be one.'

His gaze roved over her face, her hair, her shoulders and down over the curves of her breasts, and she knew she should draw her coat around herself, that she shouldn't pour any more petrol on this particular fire, yet she didn't move.

There was something powerful in his hunger. Something that made her feel as if she, the mediocre cuckoo in her aunt and uncle's nest, was beautiful and mysterious. A femme fatale who could make a man do anything. Perhaps she could make *this* man do anything.

Before she knew what she was doing, Nell leaned back slightly in her chair, allowing her coat to fall open so that the curves of her body were clearly visible beneath her clinging dress.

As she knew it would, his gaze followed those curves, igniting little fires inside her everywhere it went.

'I will be a father,' he said roughly. 'I will be anything you want. As long as you and I sleep together as much as possible. I'll have to rearrange my schedule, of course, but I can make it work.'

Sleep together as much as possible sounded good, yes—

*What are you doing? Did you fully comprehend what he's asking you to do? You didn't come here for this. You came for the sake of your baby.*

Nell gritted her teeth, attempting to put aside the heat rising inside her, trying to focus yet again on what he'd said. He would be a father. Also, there was something about a schedule…

'Schedule?' she asked. 'What schedule?'

'The schedule I use to run my life,' he said. 'My time is expensive and so I schedule every minute of it. That includes any time I take to spend with lovers. I will add the baby to the schedule and I will definitely be adding time for you.'

A little shock went through her, though she wasn't sure why. Important people were often very busy, so it made sense to have a schedule. Then again, scheduling lovers? That seemed over the top.

Aristophanes Katsaros *was* over the top though. Everything about him screamed intensity. The vivid silver of his eyes. His deep, rough voice. His compelling, electric presence. A genius. A billionaire. Head of a global finance company. Powerful. No part of him was middle-of-the-road.

And *this* man was the father of her baby.

There was such satisfaction to be had about that particular fact. That this man was her child's father and that she, as mediocre as she was, had attracted his attention.

In a dim corner of her brain, a warning sounded. Because no matter how pleased she was that he wanted her, he was also a stranger to her, despite how many times she'd had sex with him. And now he was demanding that she live in one of his houses. Demanding that she be put in his schedule so they could have sex.

What on earth was she doing even contemplating it? She'd slipped up back in the elevator and made a mistake, giving in to the power of their physical chemistry. It couldn't happen again, not given how much it clouded her thinking. She had a child to consider now and that baby was more important than anything else in her entire life.

Taking another slow breath, she dug her nails into her palms, the slight pain an antidote to the heat in her blood. 'No,' she said. 'I don't want you to schedule me for anything. And I don't want to move into one of your houses either, not when I don't even know you.'

Instantly his dark brows drew down into a scowl, the silver glitter of his eyes becoming even more intense. 'That is not acceptable,' he growled.

'Which part is not acceptable?'

'All of it.'

Nell tried to keep a grip on her temper, meeting him stare for stare, because, while she might be only a lowly kindergarten teacher and he a powerful billionaire, she couldn't let him get under her skin. Not again. He might be used to getting his way, but she wouldn't let him this time. Stubbornness of the male kind was something she was used to dealing with—in boys, admittedly, not men—but fundamentally they were the same.

She needed to hold her ground, make him understand that he wasn't in charge of this.

'I don't care if it's acceptable,' she said evenly. 'The only thing I require of you is that you be a father to this child. Be part of their life.'

'So you've already said.'

'I only wanted to make sure you heard. Little boys have painted-on ears.'

His scowl became a glower, his gaze burning like liquid mercury. 'I am not a little boy, Miss Underwood,' he said in a voice like gravel. 'Shall I demonstrate how I differ?'

More heat shot down her spine. Oh, yes, she wanted him to demonstrate. She *badly* wanted him to demonstrate. But again, she couldn't give in. Sex with him wasn't what she was here for. Because while it had been amazing, the experience in the elevator had also reminded her of why surrendering to him was a bad idea.

She'd always wanted a husband and partner, a family, a chance to recreate the family she'd lost after her parents had died. She wanted that security again, the feeling of belonging, and she already knew she wasn't going to get that with Aristophanes Katsaros.

He was rich and powerful beyond her wildest imaginings. He belonged to a world she had no conception of and didn't want to be a part of anyway. And even aside from all of that, he was also incredibly overbearing and rude. A man like that would suck her in, chew her up, and spit her out, she had no doubt.

She shifted, holding his relentless stare. The glitter of heat still burned there, but there were shadows now as well. The storm clouds of his temper, tarnishing the silver to steel.

'If you don't want me to treat you like a little boy, then you'll have to stop acting like one,' she said with an attempt at calm. 'I am not having sex with you again, and I will not be moving out of my flat, and that's final.'

His eyes darkened further. He was clearly not a man used to being denied. 'I am very rich, Miss Underwood. You do understand that, don't you? If you don't want one of my houses, then I can buy you one. I can buy you a whole town if you prefer.'

'I don't want you to buy me anything.'

'But you *do* want me to be involved in my child's life, correct?'

'Yes. I believe a child should have two parents.'

'A child always has two parents.'

Nell gritted her teeth. 'That's not what I'm asking and you know it.'

'No, I do not know it. You wished me to be involved, so here I am, involving myself.' The tension in the air around him had thickened and pulled taut, and now she could feel it reaching her, an electrical field prickling over her skin.

He leaned forward, elbows on his desk. 'What, exactly, is your objection?'

She dug her nails into her palms harder. 'I'm not upending my entire life to go and live in one of your houses. I have a job. I have friends. I don't want to leave.'

'What? That cluttered little flat?' There was an edge of disdain in his voice. 'Hardly a suitable place for a child of mine to live in. There are security issues, for a start, and also I am not in Melbourne frequently. Not only would it be safer if you and the baby were in one of my residences, it would also make visiting more efficient.'

Now it was her temper starting to rise. 'I'm not giving up my job to—'

'I will find you another job. It cannot be that hard to find something else to do.' There was an unyielding note in his voice, his gaze steel that felt as if it were running straight through her.

'But... I don't know you,' she burst out. 'Why on earth would I want to live with you when you're a complete and utter stranger to me?'

'That can be remedied.' He shoved back his chair and got to his feet in a sudden explosion of movement, stalking with animalistic grace around the side of his desk like some great hunting cat.

Stalking to her.

She half rose too, her heart beating out of control, but by then he was standing in front of her, leaning over her, bracing his hands on the arms of her chair. He stared down into her face, his expression so hungry and fierce she almost went up in flames there and then.

'Tell me you don't want me,' he demanded, low and rough. 'Tell me that sex with me isn't all you're thinking about right now.'

Her mouth had dried. All she could think about was how warm his body was, how good he smelled. How she wanted to kiss him, rip off his suit, be naked with him. Have his hot skin sliding over hers. Have his mouth on her... God, everything.

'I... I'm not.' Her voice was a mere scrape of sound.

He lowered his head until his mouth was millimetres from hers. 'Liar,' he murmured. 'You're thinking about it right now. You're thinking about that night we had together and what happened in the elevator just before. You want it again. You want more. You want me.'

His lips were so close. All she'd have to do was lift her head and they would be against hers. She could taste him again. She could feel beautiful and wanted again.

He wasn't wrong. She did want him.

'You're asking too much,' she said huskily, trying to fight him and her own desire. 'You're asking me to change my entire life for you.'

'Your life is going to change anyway, and so will mine.' He bent a touch lower, his mouth even closer. 'Spend tonight with me. Help me get rid of this chemistry. Then perhaps we can have a rational conversation.'

It was difficult to think with him so close and her body so hungry, but she tried. Spend the night with him... That didn't sound bad. And he was right that they needed to get rid of their chemistry. How could they have a discussion about their child with that getting between them and distracting them? They'd both underestimated how strong it still was.

She tried to get some moisture into her dry mouth. 'My flights... I have appointments...'

'I will handle it.' He brushed his mouth over hers in the lightest of kisses. 'I will handle everything.'

Nell shivered. She had no doubt that he would, just as he'd handled it when she'd slipped and hurt her head. He'd got her to hospital, organised a doctor, made sure she was cared for... And after all, they really did need a clear-headed discussion about the baby. He'd said he'd be a father…

His hand moved from the arm of the chair to her coat, pulling aside the fabric, then his fingertips grazed over the curve of one breast, her hip, her thigh, before lifting again, brushing down the side of her neck to her throat, settling on the frantic beat of her pulse.

'Say yes, Nell,' he murmured. 'The baby will be safe. *You* will be safe with me, I promise.'

It was strange to feel the tension slip away from her in that moment. She didn't know him, yet she believed him. In the same way as she'd reached for his hand when she'd knocked herself out that night in Melbourne. As if her body had known who he was before her mind had. Known that he wasn't a stranger to her, that she could be safe with him.

He meant what he said. So what would it hurt?

His palm was a tender weight at the base of her throat and she could feel every part of her come alive once again at his touch.

She lifted her head, brushing his mouth in a return kiss, but he pulled away, just out of reach. Her breath caught as she stared up at him, at the burning intensity of his gaze. 'Say yes,' he repeated softly. 'If you say yes, you'll get everything you want.'

His hand slid from her throat, slowly down over the curve of one breast, and cupped it gently, his thumb teasing her aching nipple through the fabric of her dress.

She trembled, arching into the warmth of his palm.

Everything she wanted…

Right now, all she could think of was him.

A long breath escaped her and she reached up, sliding her fingers in his thick black hair. It felt like raw silk against her skin. She gripped it, drawing his head down, making sure he couldn't pull away.

'Yes,' she whispered against his mouth.

'Tonight.' It was a growl. 'You'll be mine tonight.'

'Yes.'

Then his mouth was on hers and all words were lost.

# CHAPTER SIX

ARISTOPHANES TURNED OVER and opened his eyes. Half of him had been dreading that the night before had been a dream, that when he awoke he'd find his bed empty and the woman he'd been with, the warm, silky, beautiful little woman he'd spent the night exploring every inch of, would be gone.

But she wasn't gone. She was still fast asleep next to him in his giant bed, her thick auburn hair spread like kelp over the white Egyptian cotton pillowcase. Her hands were tucked beneath her chin like a child's, her auburn lashes lying still on her cheeks. The sheet had slipped down to her waist, exposing pale shoulders, the swell of her stomach and the graceful arch of her back.

She was lovely. So lovely.

Once she'd agreed to a night together the day before in his office, he'd been very tempted to simply lay her out on the carpet before his desk and have her there and then. However, he'd decided that there would be fewer interruptions if he took her back to his penthouse apartment on the Upper East Side, that looked out over Central Park.

So he had and they'd fallen into bed immediately, only surfacing for food and drink, before losing themselves in each other again. They hadn't talked. They'd let their bodies continue the same wordless conversation they'd first had back in Melbourne, communicating via sensation, with touches and licks, and caresses and bites, and pleasure.

It had been incredible. Maybe even more incredible than that first night they'd spent together, which was saying something.

He wanted to reach out and touch her, trace her little bump the way he hadn't been able to keep from doing in the elevator the day before, a rare experience for him since usually after a night with a lover, all he wanted to do was leave. Then again, they hadn't had much sleep and she was still jet-lagged. She really should have some rest.

*Especially since she's pregnant.*

An unwelcome arrow of reality pierced him, making his chest feel tight and uncomfortable. Yes, how could he have forgotten that? He was going to be a father.

It was hard thinking when he was right next to her, with her warmth and scent all around him, because she made him want to do things other than thinking. So, he slid out of bed carefully without waking her.

And he did need to think. She'd been very clear the day before that she didn't want to move into one of his residences, or give up her life in Melbourne, and why her feelings about this mattered to him, he wasn't sure. But they did, and he didn't like that they did.

Frowning to himself, he went into the en suite bathroom, stepped into the huge granite shower, and turned on the water, letting it slip over his naked body.

Logically it made sense to insist she move where it was easier for him to visit both her and the child. He could more easily care for her there—or rather have his staff care for her. Also, the more he thought about it, the more he realised he wanted his child to have one place to grow up in. A home.

He'd had one once, before his mother had abandoned him. A large house in Athens, with a garden he'd played in, but that was all he remembered about it. He remembered more of being shipped around the country, from one foster family to another, always a new house, always new family. He'd lost count of how many homes he'd had, which was why he'd used his mind to escape. In the privacy of his own head, there was familiarity, continuity. Control.

Yet while that had worked for him in many ways, he didn't want his own child to have that kind of childhood. It had been a lonely existence to be always left longing for a connection with someone, anyone. A longing that had never been fulfilled, since he'd never stayed with any family long enough to establish any kind of connection.

Eventually he'd excised that longing from his heart and taught himself not to want, never to need. But still…

His child should have better than that.

He stepped out of the shower, dried himself off and pulled on the first pair of trousers that came to hand.

Then he went out of the bedroom, padded down the hallway and into the cavernous kitchen of his massive apartment, and began the process of making coffee.

Yes, logically the child should be accessible to him and he had to be close, or at least within easy reach should anything happen with Nell. A child cared for by only one parent was a child at risk; some people, for one reason or another, couldn't deal with the pressures of parenthood after all. His mother being a prime example.

There had been times in his life when he'd tried to understand why she'd left him the way she had, but that had been the one puzzle he'd never managed to solve. There had been no signs that he could remember, no hint that she'd suddenly found being a mother to him impossible. He'd loved her and he'd thought she'd loved him.

Not that it mattered now, since he'd put his fury at her away years ago. He only wanted to be sure that the same thing wouldn't happen to his child, which meant he'd need Nell to be situated closer to him. She wouldn't like it—she'd mentioned her job and her friends—but he wouldn't be moved on this particular point. Europe, Japan, and the States were his main bases of operations, and as such he couldn't base himself in the southern hemisphere.

After preparing himself a small cup of the thick black espresso he preferred, he took it out into the living area, the huge floor-to-ceiling windows giving a fine view over the large green rectangle of Central Park far below.

Aristophanes sipped his coffee, still thinking.

He could be ruthless when he chose—he hadn't got

to where he was today by being kind or gentle—but he could offer Nell some incentives. Obviously, money wasn't going to work, since she'd told him she didn't want it, but he had plenty of other ways to leverage her agreement.

Sex, for example. One night had taken the edge off his hunger, but only slightly. He couldn't stand the thought of her going back to Melbourne right now. He wanted to keep her here, in his bed for the next few days, and, considering how passionate and wanton she'd proved herself to be, he thought she wouldn't refuse him.

She wanted him every bit as badly as he wanted her, and he was prepared to use their chemistry to get her to do what he wanted. Also, he could find her a job if that was what she needed, and as for her friends... He'd give her his private jet so she could fly them out from Melbourne whenever she liked.

She'd find that acceptable, wouldn't she?

He sipped again at his coffee, staring out through the glass, satisfaction gathering inside him. Telling his secretaries to amend his schedule to include Nell was his first order of business. In fact, he was even considering moving his morning meeting from eight to eleven, to give himself a few more hours with her.

Conversation wasn't his strongest suit, but business negotiations were. It wouldn't be difficult to change her mind about living in one of his residences. Certainly nothing a few good orgasms couldn't fix.

Speaking of which...

Inevitable physical desire began to rise again, so he

downed the rest of his coffee, put it down on a side table, and turned from the windows. He was halfway across the room to the hallway that led to the bedroom when Nell suddenly appeared.

She was wrapped in one of his sheets, her hair a glorious auburn veil around her shoulders, and he opened his mouth to tell her to get rid of the sheet, then stopped.

Her face was very pale, almost as white as the cotton wrapped around her lovely body. 'I... I...' she murmured, took a step towards him, then staggered.

A fist closed around his heart, and he was moving before he'd even thought the action through, striding over to her and sliding an arm around her waist just as her knees went out from under her. She fell against him and he caught her, holding her fast.

'Nell,' he said urgently. 'What happened? What's wrong?'

Her pale face turned against his chest, her dark eyes suddenly full of fear. 'I'm...bleeding...'

The fist around his heart squeezed tighter. The baby...

Dimly he was aware of an unfamiliar feeling, something akin to fear, but he pushed it ruthlessly aside, sweeping her up into his arms and carrying her over to the sectional sofa near the windows. He laid her gently on it as adrenaline flooded his body, the way it had the night she'd fallen over on the pavement, but this time it was even more intense. He wanted to keep hold of her, use his body as a shield against anything that would hurt her or the baby.

*His* baby.

'Hush,' he murmured. 'And lie still. I'll get help.' As he reached into the pocket of his trousers to get his phone, Nell's fingers closed around his wrist and held on tight.

'I don't want to lose the baby,' she said hoarsely, her dark eyes full of desperation. 'Please don't let me lose it.'

In that moment certainty gathered weight and solidity inside him. A determination. She would *not* lose their baby. He'd move heaven and earth, bring down the sun if need be to ensure that she wouldn't.

'You won't lose it.' He held her gaze with his so she could see his conviction. 'I'll make sure you don't.'

The fear in her eyes eased a little and she nodded, releasing his wrist.

Ten minutes and some urgent calls later, his doctor arrived and organised for Nell to be transported via helicopter to a private hospital not far from his apartment. And as she had that night in Melbourne, Nell held tight to his hand the whole way, and didn't let go even when she was rushed into an examination room in preparation for a scan.

His whole body felt tight and that fist around his heart wouldn't let go, squeezing and squeezing. And as the doctor came in and sat by the bed, murmuring reassuring things as she prepared Nell for her ultrasound, he realised with a kind of shock that the baby hadn't seemed real to him before now. It had been an idea, a concept, a fact. He hadn't thought deeply about the reality of it, because he'd been too wrapped up in Nell and their intense physical chemistry.

Now though, as the doctor spread gel on Nell's stomach and positioned the wand, the reality of his child hit him over the head with all the solidity of a cricket bat. And along with it came the choking fear that it was too late, that she might lose it.

They might both lose their child.

He stared at the monitor beside Nell's bed, holding her hand, filled with the most intense helplessness. There was nothing he could do in this moment, nothing he could say that could affect the outcome. It was out of his hands.

It reminded him so powerfully of his childhood, of watching yet another social worker walk up to the front door of whichever house he was living in at the time, knowing that she was here to take him away again. That he was going to be moved again, given to a new family, living in a new house, and that there was nothing he could do to stop it.

His jaw was so tight it ached, and he had to use every ounce of his considerable strength to force away the fear. Nell's fingers around his were tight too, holding his hand in a painful grip, and he had no idea why everything had suddenly changed.

Why he only realised now how much he wanted something when he was on the point of losing it. And he didn't know whether it was because of her or whether it had been there inside him all along, but that didn't matter.

What mattered was that he couldn't lose his child. He couldn't.

The doctor moved the wand a few times, frowning at the screen, while Nell sat in the bed, her face the colour of ashes.

'What is it?' Aristophanes demanded, his voice rough as gravel. 'Please tell me the baby is fine.'

'The baby is fine,' the doctor said calmly, still frowning as she ran the wand back over Nell's stomach. 'At least one of them is.'

Aristophanes was conscious first of a flood of relief then, hard on its heels, cold shock. 'What? What other one?'

'Oh, there's the other one.' The doctor made another pass with the wand then the frown vanished and her face relaxed. 'It was hiding. But both have got good heartbeats and don't look like they're in any distress.'

Nell's face got even whiter. 'I'm sorry, but what do you mean by "both"?'

The doctor glanced at her then at Aristophanes and smiled. 'Oh, you didn't know? There are two babies in there. Congratulations, you're having twins.'

For a long moment neither he nor Nell spoke as the words penetrated, the shock still echoing inside him.

'Twins,' Nell murmured blankly. 'We're having twins.'

'Yes,' the doctor said, turning the monitor around so they both could see. 'Do you want to know the gender?'

Aristophanes stared fixedly at the monitor and the two little pulsing heartbeats on the screen, then he glanced down at Nell, who was still holding his hand in a death grip. Her gaze met his, dark and velvety and full of shock.

Nell nodded mutely at him and he nodded at the doctor. Not that he cared about the gender of his child. Of his child*ren*. Not when he was still reeling from perhaps nearly losing one baby, unable to even get his head around the concept of two of them.

'A perfect pair,' the doctor said. 'A girl and a boy.'

That was when Nell promptly burst into tears.

A few hours later, feeling drained and not a little shell-shocked, Nell sat once again on the couch in Aristophanes' New York apartment, wrapped up in a cashmere blanket, staring at the pale carpet and wondering what on earth she was going to do.

The night before, all she'd been able to think about was him. She hadn't been able to get enough, and the more she had of him, the more she wanted. He'd been ravenous for her too, and she'd decided to allow herself the whole night of not thinking of anything else.

It had been amazing, magical. So when she'd finally woken up and gone to have a shower, she hadn't been thinking about the baby. Her head had been too full of him and what she was going to do now they'd had their night together.

She'd started to wash herself dreamily and only then had she noticed the blood. That, combined with the lack of sleep and heat of the water, had nearly made her faint. Somehow, dizzy and nauseated, she'd managed to get herself out of the shower and semi-dry, before stumbling down the hallway to the living area to find him.

Only then had she fainted.

He'd caught her though, the strength of his arms surrounding her as he'd carried her over to the couch. For a brief moment she'd felt safe and cared for. But after that...

She didn't like to think about the tense hour after that, of being rushed to a hospital and then waiting for the doctor to see if her baby was okay. She'd been numb with fear and dread, her only lifeline Aristophanes' big warm hand around hers.

She hadn't wanted to lose her baby. She couldn't bear the thought.

Finding out the baby was fine had made her dizzy with relief.

Finding out that there were two babies instead of one had been a shock. To put it mildly. Because at her first scan there hadn't been two. Apparently, though, one could remain undetected that early.

She'd felt ridiculous for bursting into tears, but the surprise of twins on top of everything else had been too much for her. Aristophanes' arms had gone around her once again, and she'd turned her face against his chest, the intellectual part of her wondering why it was that she felt so much better when she was in his arms. Especially when she knew nothing about him. Yet in that moment, she hadn't been thinking intellectually. She'd been nothing but rubbed-raw emotion as the doctor had said a lot of stuff that had gone over her head and was only now sinking in.

For the health of her babies, she had to rest. Not complete bed rest, but she had to limit her activities. No lifting heavy objects. No standing upright for longer than twenty minutes. No walking longer than twenty minutes. And definitely no sex.

Now here she was, in this stranger's apartment, expecting not one but two of his babies, and the health of those babies was dependent on a support system at home that she didn't have.

She didn't know what to do.

How was she supposed to return to Melbourne? She couldn't work, that much was certain, and she'd need someone to look after her, and, given that she had no one to do that for her, there was only one solution.

Aristophanes and his demand that she live in one of his residences.

Before he'd made her lose her mind in his office, he'd suggested it, yet she'd been barely able to take it in, too blinded by her need for him. There had been a momentary spark of temper then…well. She hadn't been able to think more about it.

Now, though, she was staring that demand full in the face.

She liked her job and her flat, and her life in Melbourne. After she'd left her aunt and uncle's house at eighteen, she'd shifted cities from Perth where she'd grown up, to Melbourne across the country, wanting to get as far away from childhood as she could. She'd been determined to make a new life for herself, in a new city where no one knew her and she wasn't bound by the limitations her aunt and uncle had put on her.

She'd always wanted to make a difference to people, to help them, and while she hadn't been smart enough for med school or nursing, or social work, being a pre-school teacher had fulfilled the nurturing, protective need in her.

No one had looked after her as a child. No one had cared after her parents had died. The kids she looked after obviously still had parents, but someone needed to watch over them during the day, and she'd be that someone.

She loved the work and didn't want to give it up. Yet there didn't seem to be a lot of choice, not if she wanted to put the health of her children first. That was if Aristophanes Katsaros' offer was still open. She assumed it was, since she was still pregnant, and he'd been very clear the day before about what he wanted. Then again, who knew? He might have changed his mind since sex was off the table.

She lifted her gaze from the carpet to where he stood in the middle of the vast minimalist living area, all pale carpet, pale walls and black leather furniture. He was pacing back and forth, talking on his phone. She wasn't sure what language he was speaking—it was too fast for her to guess—but it definitely wasn't English.

He'd told her to sit and rest while he 'organised' some things, but she hated sitting still. She also wanted to know what he was organising. She wanted to know what he thought about the fact that they were having twins.

In the hospital, his face had been set in granite lines, his whole body radiating tension. Yet his long fingers around hers had been gentle and firm, holding her with intent. He clearly hadn't been about to let her go and she'd liked that. His grip had felt like an anchor, holding her steady against a powerful current.

She'd seen fear in his eyes, though, and for some reason it had been comforting that he'd been scared for their baby too. But then had come the revelation of the twins and his eyes had gone dark with shock.

Did he want them? She didn't know. They hadn't talked about it. They hadn't talked about anything, and, despite her spending all of the previous night with him, she still knew nothing about him.

Today he was in another grey suit with a white shirt. His jacket had been thrown carelessly over one of the chairs, his shirtsleeves rolled up, exposing strong tanned forearms. Even now, after everything, her heart beat fast and her mouth dried as she looked at him move with careless, athletic grace.

What was going to happen? Whatever it was, she wasn't going to like it, she just knew. Perhaps there was another option that didn't involve throwing herself on his mercy, or upending her life, yet if one existed, she couldn't think of what it might be.

It was times like these, bad times, that she wished desperately her parents hadn't died, especially her mother. She wished she could talk to her about her pregnancy, about how she was going to be a mother too, but…that was impossible. She had only her aunt and her aunt hadn't cared. Her aunt had four other children of her own and she'd never shown much interested in her husband's brother's little girl.

For a second Nell closed her eyes, trying to recall her mother's face, but there was only a faint blur in her memory. It had been too long. All she had left now was the faint scent of her mother's favourite perfume and the gentle warmth of her hugs.

Nell's stomach hollowed, her throat feeling thick, but she forced away the rush of emotion. God, she didn't have the energy to cry again.

In front of her Aristophanes stopped pacing and pocketed his phone. 'It is arranged,' he said, striding over to where she sat.

'What's arranged?' she asked.

He came to a stop in front of her, folding his arms over his broad chest, his gaze the colour of steel. 'You will not be returning to Melbourne. At least not until our children are born.'

A little shock went through her. She hadn't known what to expect from him, but she hadn't thought he'd take charge so immediately. There was no denying the authority in his voice though, the tone of a man used to giving commands and having them obeyed.

Deep down she was conscious of something tight and afraid relaxing, but her temper flickered. He hadn't even asked her what she wanted; he'd simply decided all on his own. 'Thank you for asking my opinion,'

she said acidly. 'Always nice to have what I want completely disregarded.'

Storm clouds gathered in his eyes. 'What you want
is irrelevant. You are carrying two children—*my* children—and the best thing for their welfare and therefore
yours is to be properly cared for by me.'

Her temper, already frayed by the day's emotions,
flickered higher. She was tired. So very tired. 'They're
also *my* children,' she snapped. 'And since when did
their welfare suddenly become of the utmost importance to you?'

'Since sleeping with you almost lost them,' he
snapped right back.

Her anger leapt, and she half rose from the couch.
'So this is my—'

But before she could finish, he was suddenly there,
reaching for her and gathering her up in his arms like
a child. For a moment she lay still against the hot wall
of his chest, too surprised to move. Then her anger re-
doubled, and she twisted. 'Let me go!'

His grip on her tightened. 'Keep still,' he growled, his
stormy gaze full of steel. 'This will not help the babies.'

At that, all her fury abruptly flickered then went
out. He was right, of course. Getting angry and arguing wasn't exactly the rest the doctor had ordered. Her
children mattered more than her anger.

She took a breath, willing herself to relax. 'Fine. But
if you don't want me to argue with you, don't make me
the bad guy.'

He scowled. 'I am not making you the bad guy.'

'Yes, you did. You made it sound as though I somehow nearly lost the babies on purpose.'

'I… I did not mean that.' His mouth tightened. 'I just did not like the idea that we put them at risk for something as meaningless as sex.'

This time it was hurt that echoed through her. 'Meaningless? Is that what you think last night was?'

'It was pleasurable,' he said tightly. 'But hardly the most important thing in the world.'

The splinter of hurt slid deeper inside her. It *had* been pleasurable, he wasn't wrong about that, but it had never been meaningless, not to her. He'd made her feel, for the first time in her life, beautiful, desirable, and…special. It had deeply affected her. But clearly it hadn't been the same for him. Pleasurable, he'd said. Not that important.

Stupidly, her eyes filled with tears, which she hated. She hated, too, that somehow she'd given him the power to hurt her in this way, because what did it matter that it hadn't been as earth-shattering for him as it had been for her? Did she really care what he thought about it anyway?

Since she'd left her aunt and uncle's, she'd told herself that she didn't care about other people's opinions of her. That she was tired of caring. Tired of wanting more than she'd ever been given. Tired of feeling so insecure all the time.

Yet here she was, expecting twins with this scowling man, and she was hurt that he hadn't thought that sex with her was as great as she'd thought it was herself.

Stupid of her. She didn't care what he thought, not one iota.

'That not-very-important sex created these babies,' she said coolly, blinking away the tears and leaning her head against his shoulder. 'But I'm glad it was merely "pleasurable" for you.'

He stared down at her, his eyes narrowing, and it was downright unfair how that scowl made him look even hotter than he already was. 'You are tired,' he said abruptly. 'You were jet-lagged when you arrived, and then I kept you up far too late. You have had so little sleep and today has been full of too many surprises.' He turned and started in the direction of the hallway, still carrying her as if she weighed nothing at all. 'You should rest while I prepare everything for our trip tomorrow.'

That he was planning something else he hadn't told her about somehow didn't come as a surprise. 'What trip?' she asked as he carried her into the hallway.

'I own an island off the coast of Greece and the villa there is perfect for convalescing. There is also a separate villa where the doctor can stay should any emergencies happen.'

Of course he owned a Greek island. And apparently she was expected to stay there like Napoleon on Elba, except pregnant and without the benefits of being the Emperor of France or of having an army.

She glared up at him. 'Did you even think to ask me whether I might like to go to Greece or was this just another thing that you decided?'

'I have some meetings in Athens,' he said, stalking through into the bedroom. 'I can make sure you're safely settled while I'm there.'

'What if I don't want to go to Greece? What if I want to stay here?'

The bedroom was huge, his vast bed pushed up against one wall, the sheets tangled from their activities the night before.

'What you want is irrelevant,' he said, carrying her over to the bed. 'The well-being of the babies is all that matters.'

That hurt too. To her aunt and uncle, all she'd been was an extra and very much unwanted child, but to Sarah at the preschool, she was a valued teacher. The children she taught loved her and missed her when she wasn't there. To them she was important.

So to be treated as if she were nothing more than a human incubator now made her feel like that unwanted child once again. She hated it. She hated, too, that he was right.

'Fine. But the well-being of the babies also depends on the well-being of the mother,' she said tartly as he set her down gently on the mattress. 'And being treated as if I'm nothing more than a vessel for your children does not exactly help my well-being.'

'You are not just a vessel.' He glanced down at the small bump of her stomach, then unexpectedly he reached down and touched it, his fingers tracing the curve.

A small arrow of surprise caught at her, because, as

well as possession, there was reverence in the touch, and she hadn't expected that of him.

Then he spoiled it by straightening suddenly, his hand dropping away, storm clouds shifting in his eyes. 'Do not be difficult, Nell.'

'I'm not being difficult. You're the one being rude, hurtful and overbearing, not to mention ordering me around like a small dog.' She gripped the edge of the mattress. 'We were supposed to talk about this, remember? That's why I came here to New York in the first place, to have a conversation about what we're going to do, not for you to have a conversation with yourself.'

He was silent, clenching and unclenching his hands as if trying to relax them, and she suddenly had the impression that, for all his authority, all his apparent confidence, he was as much at sea about the situation as she was. Except he either didn't know he was at sea or couldn't admit it. And that was a surprise. He was a man used to being in charge and making decisions, and he needed to be considering the vastness of his company. He brought that natural authority to sex, too, yet she'd held her own against him there, matching him passion for passion. They'd found a natural equilibrium in bed, each of them the other's perfect match.

Out of bed, though, it was another story. He was just as stubborn as she was, and what worked with physical passion didn't work when it was two people trying to negotiate a difficult situation.

She let out a breath. Arguing wasn't going to help and she didn't want to fight him anyway. She didn't have the energy for it. But still, one thing she'd learned dealing with both children and their parents was that sometimes hammering at someone wasn't the way to go. Especially when it only made them push back even harder.

Sometimes a different approach worked better.

With a conscious effort, she pushed aside her anger. 'Look, I'm sorry. But all of this has been a terrible shock. I was hoping to talk to you, not spend the night with you. I didn't even know if you'd welcome the idea of a baby, let alone be a father to it. And then to think I was losing it, then finding out it's twins…' She swallowed. 'It's a lot to deal with.'

His steely gaze flickered, as if he'd been expecting another attack, not her sudden honesty. 'Yes,' he said after a moment. 'Yes, it is. And I admit that the situation we find ourselves in is…difficult. My schedule is full for the entire month and I do not have a lot of leeway to include you and the babies, which is why I decided on Greece. I can visit you and make sure everything is as it should be.'

Well, at least he'd made a stab at explaining his reasoning, even if it didn't make much sense to her. Especially his ridiculous schedule. If he was the boss, couldn't he rearrange a few things?

She released her grip on the mattress. 'Why is me going home to Melbourne so difficult? Surely if you're the CEO of your company, you can do whatever you want?'

'Within reason,' he said. 'But I cannot stand wasted time or inefficiency, and Melbourne is out of my way.'

'Why do you need to visit me at all? You've only known you'll be a father for all of twelve hours. Also, we can't have sex, so what's the point of a visit?'

He glowered, as if she'd pointed out something he didn't like. 'I didn't lie when I told you that the welfare of my children became important to me the moment I thought I was losing them. In that examination room, looking at that monitor and seeing two heartbeats, that's when I decided. And as you've already pointed out, the health of the babies is dependent on the health of the mother. That's why I want to visit. I need to make sure you are well.'

Nell felt that little splinter of hurt work its way even deeper inside her, which was annoying. Why did it matter to her that he visit her for *her*, not simply because she was the mother of his children? Why did she want more than that? They'd spent two nights together, that was the grand total of their dealings with each other, and, while those two nights had rocked her world on its axis, the reality of the man standing in front of her was very different from the lover who'd made her see actual stars. Perhaps too different.

'In that case,' she said tightly, 'I'd imagine it'll be a very quick visit.'

'Yes. It will. Which is another reason for you to be close to where I do business. There's no point wasting time in idle conversation.'

Nell opened her mouth to tell him he was being an absolute bastard, but abruptly she didn't have the energy. All she wanted to do now was sleep. 'Fine,' she said wearily. 'I'm sure you have plenty to do. Don't worry about me. I'll be okay.'

He kept on frowning. 'You don't seem—'

'Please, just leave me alone,' she interrupted, the frayed tether she had on her temper snapping. 'I need to sleep.'

His mouth worked, as if he meant to say something. But then, clearly changing his mind, he straightened. Gave her a single nod, then turned on his heel and went out.

# CHAPTER SEVEN

ARISTOPHANES WAITED UNTIL the rotors had slowed, then he opened the door of the helicopter, got out, then turned to help Nell disembark.

They'd just touched down on the helipad near his villa on Ithasos, a tiny green jewel of an island set in the deep turquoise blue of Mediterranean, near Mykonos.

His villa here was one of his preferred residences, and since it worked in well with his schedule for the next week, he'd decided it would be the perfect place for Nell. He'd have some time to spend helping her get settled in before he had to go on to London—he'd even managed to fit into his schedule a whole afternoon and evening to show her around his house and the island.

He knew she'd been unhappy with his decision back in New York that she should stay here for the duration of her pregnancy, but, really, it was the best solution for both of them. He didn't want her going back to Melbourne on her own, not when he had no idea of what kind of support she had there, and not when he couldn't accompany her because of his schedule—after the near miss with the babies, he didn't want to let her out of his sight if he could help it. Which meant taking her to Greece was the most logical decision, especially given her pregnancy restrictions.

He could have asked her, he supposed, as she'd flung at him back in New York, but then she'd argued anyway, and arguing was a waste of time. Especially when he'd already decided what was going to happen.

The potential loss of the babies had pierced him in a place he hadn't known he was vulnerable, a painful place. A place of fear. It was true what he'd told her, that he hadn't realised how badly he'd wanted those children until he'd nearly lost them.

Before leaving New York, he'd talked to Cesare on the phone for a long time about how Nell was pregnant and that it was twins. His friend had taken a good deal of amusement from that particular fact, but Aristophanes saw nothing amusing about it. Almost to his own surprise, when he'd told Nell he'd keep them safe, he'd meant it. He'd meant it more than he'd meant anything else in his entire life. The children were not abstracts any longer, not ideas. Not equations or problems to solve, but small lives under threat, lives that were precious. He would never allow them to be lost, which meant he'd do everything in his power to make sure that didn't happen. Even if it meant making decisions that Nell didn't like.

*You didn't have to be so cold though.*

The thought was an uncomfortable one and it had nagged at him ever since they'd left New York. It was true he'd been less…kind to her than he should have, and yes, probably cold. He'd just been operating on a threat response level, which didn't allow for anyone's feelings.

When he'd implied, for example, that the sex had been meaningless in comparison to the health of the babies, there had been a flicker of what he suspected was hurt in her gaze. The same when she'd asked what the point of him visiting her was, and he'd responded with the truth, to make sure she and the twins were healthy.

It had made him wonder what it was about what he'd said that had been painful for her. Certainly with the latter, it was almost as if she'd wanted him to visit her for *her*, which was odd when, as she kept saying to him, they were complete strangers. He didn't know her and she didn't know him.

Also, he was a billionaire financial genius and she was a preschool teacher. What on earth would they have to talk about? Sex had been the language they'd used for all their communications up to this point, and if they couldn't have sex then the only other reason to bother with a visit was for health reasons.

*But why not make the effort? How can you know that you don't have anything to talk about, when you haven't bothered to initiate any kind of conversation?*

The thought sat uncomfortably inside him as he turned to help her out of the machine. Her gaze was shuttered, giving him nothing, the way it had been ever since they'd left New York. He didn't like it. It made his chest get tight, made him wonder if he'd done something wrong, made the wrong move. He didn't like that either.

Nell was pale, with circles under her eyes, her hair

flowing in thick auburn waves down her back, and she wore a pair of stretchy black pants and a loose sweatshirt in vivid emerald green. The colour made her eyes even darker, bringing out the red sparks in her auburn hair.

An inevitable punch of desire hit him as his hand settled on her hip to help her out of the helicopter, the feel of her so warm and soft, it was all he could do not to squeeze her gently then slide his hand between her thighs, see how warm and soft she was there too.

But he couldn't do that, not without endangering his children, so, with an effort that cost him far more than it should, he crushed the urge. It shouldn't still be so strong after their night in New York, yet it was, which meant yet more decisions needed to be made about what would happen after the babies were born. He already had a few ideas…

'Welcome to Ithasos,' he murmured as he helped her down onto the helipad.

The expression on her face remained guarded, her mouth tight. 'Thank you.'

She was still putting distance between them, clearly, and his patience for it was running thin. In his arms, she'd been unguarded and passionate, her dark eyes glowing with heat and desire, awe and wonder.

But now… Her lashes fell, veiling her gaze, and she turned her head away from him, shutting him out. A salty sea breeze lifted her hair from her shoulders, blowing it around her face, and again he experienced a fierce urge to touch her, push that recalcitrant lock of hers back behind her ears. Then maybe demand that she look at him, tell him why she was shutting him out.

He'd never wanted to know what someone else was thinking before, never been almost desperate to know. Yet he found himself staring at her, wishing he could see what was going on inside her lovely head.

Then the wind blew a lock of her hair across the sleeve of his suit, the strands gleaming red against the dark wool, and his thoughts shifted and changed. Would their children have auburn hair and dark eyes like hers, or would they have grey eyes like his? Would they be lovely, like her, or—?

*Emotionally dead like you?*

He gritted his teeth and forced the thought away. He had no idea where it had come from. He wasn't emotionally dead; he just preferred his emotions to be tightly controlled, which wasn't the same thing.

Their children would never be emotionally dead anyway, not with passionate Nell for a mother.

*She could leave them, though, the way your mother left you.*

Aristophanes slid his hand beneath her elbow and gripped it, mentally crushing the irrational fears that kept winding through his brain.

The children would be fine and Nell would be an excellent mother. She worked with small children after all.

Together, they walked up the white shell path that led from the helipad to the villa, threading through the olive groves that surrounded the house, along with lemon trees and lavender and other shrubs that grew well in the dry, rocky soil.

The villa itself was white plaster and on several levels, with windows that looked out over the sea, and large vine-covered terraces accessible by wide curving stone stairs. There was a pool area beside one wing of the house, with an infinity pool and sun loungers scattered about. He'd decided to put her in the bedroom next to it so she could access it more easily. A pool would be cooling and provide some nice gentle exercise.

She stayed silent as he showed her into the villa, introducing her to his housekeeper and some of the other staff, then, while the staff dealt with the luggage, he took her on a tour of the property, periodically checking on the time to make sure it would take no longer than twenty minutes as per the doctor's orders.

First, the wide salon, with doors that opened all the way out onto the terrace. Then down some stairs to the guest wing, with the big bedroom next to the pool and a wooden bed piled high with pillows. A big bathroom with a wide white porcelain bath she could lie in, and a large shower to stand beneath if she so chose.

As they came out of the bathroom, Nell went past him and over to the windows near the bed, looking out over the deep blue green of the sea. She hadn't spoken a word since they'd got out of the helicopter.

Impatience ran through him. Did she like it here? Was the bedroom to her taste or would she prefer another? He wanted to know what she thought of the island, which was strange, because why did he care about her opinion?

He'd never cared about the opinions of others before. Then again, maybe it wasn't so strange. As she'd told him, her well-being was important to the lives of their children, and if he was going to look after her, then that was his responsibility too.

*Not just her physical well-being. Her emotional well-being too.*

Another thing he'd never been concerned about before—a person's emotional well-being. And why would he? When no one had ever considered his? Yet he was considering it now. On the plane on the way over, he'd been doing a lot of reading, research papers on pregnancy mainly, and he'd discovered that the emotions of the mother did affect her foetus, and if she was, say, depressed, then the baby had worse outcomes.

He didn't want that for her or for their children.

'Will this be adequate?' he asked at last, breaking the thick silence.

She didn't turn from the window. 'Yes.' The word sounded colourless. 'It's fine.'

He frowned, taking in the elegant curve of her obdurate back, a sudden frustration rising in him. Was this all he was going to get from her? Just this…silence?

*Are you surprised? It's not as if you've given her anything but dismissal.*

A memory gripped him then, of the hurt in her eyes as she'd said what was the point of a visit without sex, and he'd implied that the health of their children was more important. Which it was, but still… They were strangers, and yet…they weren't. He'd touched every inch of her body, he knew the feel of her, the taste of her. He knew what she looked like when she came, the noises she made when he gave her pleasure. He knew her kiss, the touch of her hand, the way her nails dug into his back...

He didn't know her mind, though, and perhaps he should. Especially when she was their children's mother and they'd be raising those children together.

'Do you need food?' he asked, at a loss for what else to say, but wanting to say something to break the ice. Small talk, though, had never been his friend.

'No, thank you.' She was scrupulously polite and still didn't turn.

'Perhaps you would like to rest?' He took a couple of steps towards her. 'The bed is very comfortable.'

'I'm sure it is.'

His jaw felt tight and he didn't know what else to say. Words were always a barrier. They got in the way, imperfect and inexact, a primitive vehicle when it came to expressing ideas and concepts. Apart from sex, though, he didn't know what other tools he could use to express himself. Mind to mind would be so much easier, and it was a constant aggravation to him that no one had yet invented telepathy.

If sex hadn't been forbidden, he would simply have crossed the space between them, taken her into his arms, kissed her thoroughly, then given her all the pleasure he was capable of to make her feel better.

But he couldn't.

So he stood there uselessly, impatient and annoyed

with himself, until she finally turned around. 'I'm sorry?' she said coolly. 'Don't you have other places to be?'

'I want to know if you need anything,' he said, irritated by how inarticulate he was being, and how it almost made him feel stupid. Which he wasn't in any regard.

'I don't.' Her gaze was very level, telling him nothing.

'Do you like the villa?' he demanded, getting even more irritated with himself.

'Yes, it's fine. I said that already.'

'But do you—?'

'It's fine, Mr Katsaros,' she repeated, her voice cold as a splinter of ice.

'Aristophanes,' he growled, realising all of a sudden that she'd never said his name out loud, not once. 'You can't call me Mr Katsaros. Not when we will be having children together.'

At last, to his enormous satisfaction, tiny sparks of temper glittered in her eyes. The satisfaction was akin to when he gave her an orgasm, but sharper somehow. He liked that he could disturb her, that he could affect her in some way.

'I'm not calling you Aristophanes,' she said with some irritation. 'It's ridiculous and far too long.'

He glared at her. 'How dare you—?'

'I'll call you Dylan, after one of the naughtiest boys in my class.'

'You will *not* be calling me Dylan,' he forced out through gritted teeth.

Nell tilted her head and abruptly he realised that it wasn't only temper in her eyes, but something else, almost like…amusement. 'Bear, then,' she said. 'He's the second naughtiest and you're certainly bad-tempered enough to be a bear.'

'Bear?' he repeated blankly. 'You have a boy in your class called Bear?'

'Yes,' she said. 'So, thank you, Bear. That will be all.'

Nell watched Aristophanes' dark brows plunge into yet another one of his sexy scowls and felt extremely pleased with herself. It was a strange thing to discover that she could render this powerful, apparently humourless, billionaire genius speechless. Not to mention annoyed. And he was definitely both now, his mouth tight, his grey gaze thunderous.

It was satisfying. That she could get under his skin so easily made her feel better about being here, on this Greek island that she hadn't asked to be brought to and would effectively be imprisoned on for the next five months.

She'd thought that nothing she said would move him, since it appeared he didn't care about her at all, except that she was the mother of his children.

And she'd thought that the case all the way over from New York, on the interminable flight to Athens, where he'd spent the majority of time either staring fiercely at his laptop or reading one of the hard science magazines he'd brought with him.

Then he'd showed her into the bedroom of this admittedly very pretty villa, on this admittedly very beautiful Greek island, and she'd thought he'd show her to the bedroom then leave immediately, yet he hadn't. He'd asked inane questions instead, wanting her opinion on the villa, wanting to know if she needed anything to eat, or if she needed rest. And even when she'd said no, he'd continued to stand there, looking incredibly annoyed yet resolutely not leaving.

She had to admit it was slightly amusing that such a self-proclaimed genius could be so inarticulate, and it made the bleak feeling in her heart feel a little less bleak. He was just a man, after all. As flawed as any other.

'You can't call me Bear,' he growled.

'Why not? You do growl a lot.'

He looked typically thunderous. 'I do not.'

She expected him to simply turn around and leave then, yet he didn't. He only stood there, glaring at her accusingly. And she had the odd impression that he didn't actually want to go. He was lingering here because he wanted to talk to her.

Nell studied him a moment. Was that what he wanted? And he just didn't know how? Seemed strange for a man who'd repeatedly told her that he liked having conversations with women. Then again, those women were also very smart, weren't they? And perhaps their conversations were smart also? Perhaps he didn't have normal, casual conversations. Perhaps he didn't know how.

'Didn't you ever have a nickname when you were a little boy?' she asked, after a moment. 'Or did everyone go around calling you Aristophanes?'

'No one called me anything as a little boy.'

'No one? Not even your parents?'

'I was raised in foster care,' he said. 'I was never with a family long enough to be called anything but "boy".'

Shock prickled over her skin. She hadn't expected him to reveal anything personal about himself, still less something so sad. Or so relatable. Because if he'd been in foster care, that meant something had happened to his parents and she knew all about that.

'Oh, I'm sorry,' she said impulsively. 'I lost my parents, too. I didn't go into foster care though. I was raised by my aunt and uncle.'

His gaze sharpened. 'You were lucky.'

Nell shook her head. 'No, I wasn't. I already had four cousins and my aunt and uncle didn't want another kid. I don't know why they took me in. My uncle only said it was because he owed my dad, but he made it clear it wasn't something *he* wanted. My aunt wasn't happy either. They just kind of ignored me.'

There was a steely glint in Aristophanes' eyes. 'Ignored you? How the hell did they ignore you?'

She shrugged. 'They just did. All my cousins were six feet tall and blonde. Sporty. Academically gifted. And I was…none of the above.'

'So, what happened?'

'What do you mean what happened?'

'I mean, how did it affect you? What did you do?'

It seemed a genuine question and, since he still hadn't left, and the sharp intensity of his gaze hadn't moved from hers, she had to assume it was.

'I...decided to carve out my own identity and my own existence, I guess,' she replied. 'I wanted to be a doctor, or maybe a nurse, but I wasn't academically gifted. I wanted to care for people, especially kids, because of my own experience, I suppose. So, I moved from Perth to Melbourne, and eventually decided on preschool care. I got a few certificates, found myself a job...and the rest, as they say, is history.'

He was still staring at her as if he'd never heard of anything more mystifying in his entire life yet was determined to understand. It made that horrible, bleak feeling inside her start to fade a little. 'Why?' he demanded. 'Why did you think you weren't academically gifted? Why did you want to care for children?'

'Are we having a proper conversation now?' The words slipped from her without her thinking, the urge she had to tease him irresistible. 'Is that what's happening?'

His eyes narrowed. 'Why is that amusing? I want to know.'

'As an aside, do you ever find anything funny?'

'I haven't found anything in life to be particularly amusing, no.'

Her throat tightened abruptly. He looked quite serious. 'Well, that's a tragedy.'

Something glittered in his eyes for a moment, then it was gone. 'Tell me why,' he insisted.

She sighed. 'I thought I wasn't academically gifted because I wasn't as intelligent as my cousins. They all got straight As while I was a steady C—B plus if I was lucky—student. I never excelled in anything, and I certainly didn't have the marks I needed to be a doctor or a nurse.'

He shoved his hands in his pockets, his shoulders still tense and stiff. 'Perhaps the school you went to wasn't a good one. Perhaps the style of teaching didn't suit you.'

This time it was her turn to look at him in puzzlement. 'Or maybe I'm just not smart enough. Why is that important?'

The muscle in his jaw flicked again. 'You're the mother of my children and intelligence is important to me. Perhaps you are smarter than you think you are.'

'Or maybe I'm as dumb as a post.' The words were tinged with a bitterness she'd thought she'd long since put behind her, and she wished she hadn't said them.

He stared at her a second, then abruptly came across the room to her, still scowling ferociously as if she'd done something to offend him. 'You are not,' he said with some insistence. 'I always wondered why I wanted you so badly. The women I take as lovers are all, without exception, gifted with high intelligence. But you're not a professor or a scientist. You teach small children. But you must be very gifted in some way in order to—'

'Or maybe you want me to be smart because you can't think of any other reason to want me?' she interrupted, her temper rising. 'Children are important. They're the society we'll have one day, so why are you looking down on my profession? I'm making sure that future society will be full of people who are empathetic and understanding. Who listen. Who build good relationships with others. It's not rocket science, but it's just as important, if not more so.'

He was silent a moment longer, then the hard lines of his face eased, as if she'd proved something to him. 'There,' he said softly. 'You see? You don't think you're as dumb as a post at all.'

Her cheeks heated and she had to glance away to hide the strange fluttering feeling in her stomach that definitely didn't have anything to do with her pregnancy. 'You didn't seem to think being a preschool teacher was so great compared to being a professor or scientist. Or a mathematical genius.'

'I didn't,' he said. 'But maybe I need to change my mind.'

'Why?' She glanced at him. 'Because of me?'

'Yes.'

'But how can you say that when you don't know me?'

'Perhaps I should know you.' He kept on staring at her as if she were a puzzle he desperately wanted to solve. 'You're the mother of my children. Don't you think you're worth knowing?'

*You're not, not to a man like him. Mediocre, remember? That's what you'll always be.*

The thought drifted through her brain, thorny and sharp. It wasn't anything her aunt and uncle had ever told her outright, but their silence when it came to her had left a void. A void that her own thoughts had filled for her. Because there had to be a reason that they'd never been interested in her. Never asking her if she'd done her homework, never wanting to know which part she'd got in the school play. Never remembering her birthday and never asking to see her school reports. Never really asking her about herself at all.

She'd been forgotten. She'd always thought that maybe it was because she wasn't that interesting. Nothing special about her, nothing that would catch anyone's attention. She'd tried not to listen to those thoughts, tried to prove to herself that she was better than what her aunt and uncle thought, that she was intelligent and strong and special. But she'd never really believed it.

Not until Aristophanes had come to her the night she'd hit her head, because he hadn't been able to stay away. Then he'd given her the most perfect night she'd ever had, and for that brief time she'd believed. She'd believed she was as special as he made her feel.

She looked up into his cool silver eyes. 'You tell me. Do you want to know me purely for the sake of the babies? Or for yourself?' She wasn't sure she wanted to know the answer to that question, but it had to be asked. For her own peace of mind if nothing else.

'What difference would that make?'

'It wouldn't in the greater scheme of things. But it would make a difference to me.'

'You don't think you're worth it,' he said slowly, staring at her intently, as if she were a difficult text he was translating. And it was not a question.

The heat in her cheeks intensified and a desperate vulnerability crawled through her, making her turn her head to look out of the window so she didn't have to look into his eyes. She didn't like that he'd managed to see that about her. Then again, should she really have been so surprised? He was a genius, while she…

His thumb and forefinger gripped her chin, forcing her gaze back to his. 'Look at me,' he ordered softly. 'Is that what this is about?'

Unable to pull away, Nell could do nothing but stare back. 'I mean, would you think you were worth knowing? If no one in your entire life had ever shown any interest in you?' She threw the words at him almost defiantly.

He scowled again, but this time she had the odd sense that it wasn't her he was angry with. '*I* am showing an interest,' he said flatly. 'And if I am showing an interest then, yes, you are definitely worth knowing.'

A quiver ran through her, almost a tremble. 'But only because I'm the mother of your children. Not for any other reason, right?'

'Wrong.' His grip on her chin tightened. 'I want to know for myself. You are a puzzle, Nell. And I like puzzles. I like puzzles very much.' His thumb stroked her chin and before she could move, he'd bent his head and his mouth brushed over hers.

A shock of desire went through her and she couldn't stop herself from kissing him back, because she was hungry for this. For him.

He allowed the kiss for a second, then pulled away. 'No,' he murmured, his breathing fast. 'No, we can't do this.' He released her and stepped back. 'Rest now. I will

have the housekeeper unpack your things. But tonight...'
His gaze intensified. 'You will tell me everything about
yourself over dinner, understand?'

# CHAPTER EIGHT

ARISTOPHANES PACED OVER to the edge of the stone terrace and spent a moment gazing out over the olive groves and the darkening sea beyond Ithasos' cliffs. The sun was going down, washing the sky in oranges and pinks and reds, an evening breeze carrying the scents of the sea and sun-warmed rock, and pine.

He glanced back at the table that stood underneath the vine-covered pergola. He'd had his housekeeper prepare and arrange the table just so, setting the scene for dinner with Nell, the island scenery and sunset a perfect backdrop.

It was all as it should be and he was pleased.

After the conversation they'd had in her bedroom on their arrival, he'd been thinking. In fact, he'd spent the whole afternoon thinking. About her and what she'd said. About her childhood and how she clearly didn't view herself as being smart or intelligent or any of the things she thought she should be. Then teasing him with that silly nickname—'Bear', of all things—and then disagreeing with him about the importance of her job.

Telling him why it was important, her dark eyes glowing with conviction…

He'd felt angry at her aunt and uncle for making her think things about herself that weren't true, and then he'd been angry at himself for doing the same thing, because it was clear he had. He'd been less than complimentary about her job, but that was because he didn't know anything about it, nor had he thought about it until she'd told him what it meant.

He liked intelligence in a woman, but he was beginning to see now that it was a very specific sort of intelligence. An academic intelligence, logical and cool. Nell wasn't like that at all, but when she looked at him sometimes, he felt as if she knew things he didn't. Mysterious things he couldn't even conceive of, that made him uncomfortable and yet fascinated him at the same time.

She *was* smart, but not in the way he'd always thought about it.

That she seemed to doubt that she was worth knowing, though, had appalled him. He didn't know why it mattered, or why he felt so strongly about it, but he did. Perhaps because it was that she was the mother of his children and he didn't want her upset…

No. That wasn't the reason and he had to be honest with himself. It mattered to him because he didn't want her to think that way about herself. Because it hurt her, and he didn't like her being hurt. It also wasn't true.

He was interested in her and he was a genius, so of course she was worth knowing.

The way her mind worked intrigued him, and also

she'd been brought up by people who didn't value her, yet she'd defied them. She'd left her home, gone across the country to a new city, and found a fulfilling life despite them. That spoke of a bravery and determination, and a strength of character he found admirable.

He wanted to know more, much more. Even though being near her and not being able to do more than kiss her was a constant test of his control. Really, he should be absenting himself, taking the helicopter back to Athens for the night, not staying here, so close to temptation.

But he wasn't going to. He wanted to do something nice for her, do something to make her happy since her well-being was his responsibility now, and he didn't think she'd appreciate being abandoned so soon after arriving here.

So he'd organised everything like one of his dates, with dinner and conversation, and then they'd go to bed separately. Not exactly what he wanted, but that was the way it would have to be for the moment.

It was an interesting situation and one he'd never been in before.

Just then, Nell appeared in the doorway of the living area, stepping out through the French doors and onto the stone terrace. Her hair was curling in thick waves over her shoulders, and for once she wasn't wearing a clinging dress, but a loose, cool-looking white linen caftan. It hid her body, including her little bump, but the wide neckline almost hung off one shoulder, revealing an expanse of creamy skin that made his fingers itch to touch it.

Ignoring the urge, he strode over to the beautifully set table and pulled out a chair for her. 'Please,' he invited. 'Sit.'

She hesitated, then came over to the chair and sat down, the sweet scent of her hair and body surrounding him for a moment, making his mouth water. Knowing that he couldn't take her to bed later seemed to make the desire sharper, deeper, and he had to fight to force it away.

Resolutely steeling himself, he pushed her chair back in and moved around the table to his own opposite hers, before sitting. The candles he'd ordered leapt and twisted in their glass holders, radiating a shifting golden glow. She looked beautiful in that glow, her skin gilded, her hair gleaming with red fire.

'This is lovely,' she said, glancing around at the candles, the light glittering off the crystal glasses, silver cutlery, and the elegant glass vase with sprigs of jasmine in it. 'Did you do all this?'

'My housekeeper did, but I decided to make an event of it, yes.' He stared at her, unable to take his eyes off her. 'This is just the setting though. The true beauty here is you.' It felt natural to compliment her, even though he'd never been one for compliments, and he got his reward when she blushed, her lashes falling, her mouth curving.

He knew sensual satisfaction. He experienced it whenever he made her gasp aloud. But right here, right now, he knew another kind of satisfaction that wasn't sexual. It was a pressure in his chest and the way his mouth wanted to curve as if her smile and the obvious pleasure she'd taken from his compliment made him want to smile too.

Emotional satisfaction. He couldn't recall ever feeling anything like it. Perhaps once when that little cat he'd tried to adopt had first started lapping at the milk he'd brought her. And perhaps again the first time she'd curled up in his lap, purring as he'd stroked her. Satisfied that his presence had made a difference to another living creature's life. That he'd given them some kind of emotional pleasure.

It was the most curious feeling. Addictive, even.

Nell's lashes lifted, her dark eyes flickering with gold from the candlelight. 'I've decided something, Bear. I've decided that if you want to know everything about me, I want to know everything about you, too.'

That seemed logical and yet…he was conscious of a vague reluctance. His past wasn't a secret, and he wasn't ashamed of it, so he shouldn't feel…uneasy at the prospect of telling her. Then again, perhaps that had more to do with her clear-eyed gaze and that way she looked at him, as if she could read his mind.

He didn't like it, not at all. It unsettled him, made him feel as if he were an open book that she could read with impunity.

But he was *not* an open book. He kept his thoughts hidden, his emotions under control. They had no place in the mathematical world, the world of algorithms and money, and he liked it that way. He *wanted* it that way.

Yet he couldn't deny that, if she gave him pieces

of herself, he would have to reciprocate. Perhaps he wouldn't have thought that three months ago, but he did now. She wasn't one of his dates, after all, but the mother of his children, and maybe it would even be a good thing if she knew his background. That would help her understand the things he *didn't* want for them. He certainly didn't want, for example, the kind of childhood Nell had grown up in for them. Not abusive, but traumatising in its own way.

'Very well,' he said, reaching across the table for the jug of home-made lemonade that sat next to the bottle of his favourite red wine. 'What would you like to know?' He poured the lemonade into a heavy cut-glass tumbler and pushed it over to her, before pouring himself some wine.

'You mentioned being brought up in the foster system.' She reached for the tumbler, took a careful sip, then looked at him in sudden delight. 'Oh, this is very good!'

Again, satisfaction tugged at him, that she was pleased with what he'd given her. It made his chest burn. He tried to ignore the feeling, but his mouth twitched all the same. 'Lemonade,' he said. 'My housekeeper makes it from the lemons in our grove.' He nodded to a small bowl in the middle of the table next to some fresh bread. 'That is olive oil from our olive groves.'

'Looks amazing.' She reached for the bread, tore a piece off it, then dunked an edge into the olive oil before taking a bite. 'Mmm… And tastes amazing too.'

'My housekeeper is an amazing woman.'

'She is.' Nell leaned forward, elbows on the table as she tore off another chunk of bread. 'Okay, so tell me about you, Bear.'

Bear yet again. She seemed wedded to it, which was ridiculous. Then again, a part of him liked it. Cesare called him Ari, but that was as close to a nickname as he'd ever had. He'd never been a man to invite anything more intimate than that.

Bear, though, he could live with.

'I was born in Athens,' he said. 'I never knew my father. He and my mother split up before I arrived. I don't remember much from my time with her, but we had a large house in the hills. It had a garden. My mother was kind and loving—I never knew a moment's unhappiness. Then one morning she took me to church and left me there.'

Nell, in the process of dunking more bread in the oil, went still. 'What do you mean left you there?'

'At the end of the service, she told me to sit still in the pew and she'd be back soon, so I did. Except she didn't come back.'

Nell's eyes widened. 'What? You mean, not ever?'

'Not ever,' he confirmed, picking up his wine glass and leaning back in his chair. 'I was eight. Eventually the priest came over and asked me my name, and why I was sitting there. To cut a long story short, they eventually discovered that my mother had gone. The house was empty, there was no sign of her. I had no surviving grandparents, no other family, so I was made a ward of the state.'

A crease formed between her brows, her eyes dark and soft with what he very much hoped was *not* pity. 'Oh, that's awful,' she murmured. 'How could she have left you?'

A question he'd asked himself many times. A question he would never know the answer to.

Aristophanes lifted a shoulder. 'The why isn't relevant, only that she did. So I went into the foster system and my experience was…imperfect, to say the least. I never stayed long with a particular family. I was always being shifted around. Eventually, I decided I'd had enough. I'd taken part-time jobs here and there while I was at school, and I'd managed to save quite a bit of money. I made a few astute investments and soon found I had a knack. I'd always loved mathematics as well, and the two seemed to go together for me. That was the start of my company.'

She stared at him as if fascinated, making the pressure in his chest take on a kind of warmth and this time he liked the way she looked at him. He liked it a lot.

'You must have been very determined to leave all of that behind,' she said.

'Oh, I was. I wanted to leave my childhood behind, make my mark. I also liked numbers and the idea that you could make money with numbers. Money, too, is an interesting idea. You have physical money, obviously, but much of it exists in the ether. You have some, you lose some, you get more… It doesn't really matter, because it wasn't real to start with.'

'I know plenty of people who would disagree with you.'

'Of course. I'm talking about the idea of money, you understand. That's not really real or tangible, but the effects of it are. I like making it, I like controlling it, and I like doing things with it. It's a game.'

She leaned her chin in her hand. 'But it's not really about the money, is it?'

The question was unexpected and it made him think. 'No,' he said. 'It's not.'

Nell stared at him through the flickering candlelight. 'What is it about, then?'

'Challenging my mind, my intellect.'

'Why is that so important to you?' she asked. 'Genuine question.'

'Because there I have the most control,' he said slowly. 'I am the master of it. The numbers do what I say and on the rare occasions they don't, I make them.'

'Control is important to you?'

He shifted uncomfortably, finding the conversation vaguely unsettling. 'Yes.'

'I suppose it would be, considering how little control you had over your early life.'

'The past is irrelevant,' he said, a touch irritated and not bothering to hide it. 'It doesn't bother me. I didn't have a family, it's true, but I didn't need one. I only needed what I found in my own head to survive, and I did.'

The crease between her brows deepened and he didn't like the expression on her face, the pity in it. 'It sounds very lonely,' she murmured.

He shrugged. 'As I said, I survived. Your childhood doesn't sound any better, either, yet you survived too.'

'I did.' She took another sip of her lemonade. 'But when I said it must have been lonely, what I meant was I can relate to that. Because mine was. Not that no one spoke to me or anything, it was more having no one notice that you were maybe a bit quiet today. Or that you were pale. Or that you looked happy. The feeling that you could just...not exist and no one would ever notice you were gone.'

A sharp and painful feeling threaded through him, as if she'd touched on an old and still festering wound. *You felt that too.*

He had. Once. He didn't feel it now, though, because he couldn't not exist without someone knowing, because everyone knew who he was. He'd made sure everyone knew. So any pain he felt now was merely an echo, phantom-limb pain from a part of himself he'd cut out years ago. As was the anger that used to overcome him every now and then, formless and hot, with seemingly no cause.

He hadn't felt that for at least a decade, not since he'd poured everything of himself into his business, using his ambition as the engine that drove his life. He'd needed a purpose and his life of numbers and money was it. That was why he had his schedule, so every second of his life was dedicated to using his intellect in the most efficient way and not getting sidetracked by...anything else.

'People would notice,' he said tersely. 'They'd certainly notice if you were gone.'

Her gaze was very dark and she looked at him steadily, and for a second there was pain in her gaze. 'Who would?'

At first he thought it might be another tease, but no, not with the way she was looking at him now, not with that pain. She really wanted to know.

'*I* would,' he said. 'I would notice you were gone and the world would be a poorer place for it.'

He meant it. She could see the force of his conviction in his steel-grey eyes, and a small hot glow started up in the centre of her chest.

At first, she'd wished the words back, because it had sounded too needy, too desperate. Yet he hadn't treated it that way at all.

She could feel the tension between them again, the force of their chemistry and the need in his eyes that he didn't hide from her. But they couldn't act on it, not with the health of their children at stake. 'You shouldn't say such things to me,' she said quietly.

'Why not?' His gaze didn't flicker. 'It's true.'

'Is it? You can't sleep with me, remember?'

'You think I'd only say that to sleep with you?'

She felt too vulnerable staring at him the way she was doing, but she was the one who'd started this conversation. The one who'd told him about her aunt and uncle, revealing much more than she'd meant to. She couldn't falter now. 'I don't know—would you?'

A spark of temper glittered in his eyes. 'I do not need

to give a woman empty compliments to get her to sleep with me. I never give empty compliments, full stop.'

Of course, he wouldn't. He wasn't that kind of man. Every word he spoke was with intention and purpose, because he meant it. Which then must mean…

*He was telling the truth about you.*

She swallowed, her mouth dry. 'You really do think those things? That the world would be a poorer place without me?' Sometimes, in her darker moments, she'd wondered if anyone would care if she simply ceased to exist. Sometimes, she couldn't think of one person who'd care.

Aristophanes' gaze was almost ferocious. 'Of course it would. Your beauty is incomparable, and I have never wanted anyone the way I want you.'

'But those are just physical—'

'I haven't finished,' he interrupted sharply. 'You're also strong and determined, and very stubborn. Which is annoying, but you stand up for what you believe in and you've never once let me intimidate you, which is a feat, considering I am much more powerful than you are.' He paused a moment. 'I wondered if perhaps you would be like my mother, but you aren't. You would never abandon your child to its fate, which means you will be an excellent mother to our children. Also…' His gaze intensified. 'You are very perceptive, and I think you have far more intelligence than you give yourself credit for.'

Something quivered in her, something deep inside. It was ridiculous. She didn't need a man's praise to make her feel good about herself, yet it was *his* praise that made her feel as though she really was all those things he'd said. Not just any man, but him in particular.

*You will be an excellent mother...*

She'd wondered on and off, after she'd found out she was pregnant, whether she, who'd had so little love in her life, could even be a good mother. Whether she'd know how to show them how much they mattered, how important they were, and how much she loved them. She'd tried not to think about it though, because if she did, the doubt would eat her alive. Now she felt it like a fault line running through an essential part of her.

'You really think I would?' she couldn't help asking, hating how needy she sounded and yet not being able to stay silent. 'Make a good mother, I mean?'

'I think,' he murmured, 'that a woman with as much to give as you have will make the most wonderful mother any child could ask for.'

Nell's cheeks burned and she had to look away at last, unable to hold his gaze. She didn't want to negate his praise by dismissing it or minimising it, but she wasn't used to compliments, especially about her most deeply held doubts, and couldn't think of a word to say.

In the end all she managed was, 'Thank you. That actually...means a lot to me.'

A weighted silence fell.

She hadn't realised until arriving here that the bleak feeling in her heart dogging her since leaving New York had been loneliness and doubt. And now he'd lightened that load somehow. Even though he'd insisted on her coming here, he'd taken time out of his schedule to show her around and then have dinner with her and while it might not seem like much, from what he'd told her about his schedule and about himself, she had the feeling that this was a big deal for him.

Perhaps he was lonely too. His childhood had certainly sounded as bleak as hers, probably bleaker since at least she'd had some sense of continuity with her cousins and aunt and uncle. But he'd had no one. No one at all.

Finally Nell lifted her lashes and looked at him again.

He'd leaned forward, elbows on the table, his wine in front of him, watching her. His grey gaze seemed unreadable and yet she could see the silver glitter of hunger there. Hunger for her, she knew, but that wasn't news. She knew all about his physical hunger. However, now she suspected that there might be something more underneath that. Not sexual hunger, but a hunger for something deeper and more profound.

He was a man who prized his intelligence, his mind. A cerebral man, yet one who also enjoyed his physical hungers. But his emotional hungers… Did he know about those? Did he ever acknowledge them or understand them?

*You know he doesn't.*

No, she was beginning to see that. And maybe that was where her power lay. She could see things in him that he couldn't see himself. She knew things about him that he didn't know.

*He's lonely. Profoundly lonely.*

The thought ripped a hole in her heart.

'If you don't have family, who do you have, then?' she asked softly. 'Friends? Colleagues?'

He lifted one powerful shoulder. 'I have one friend in Italy whom I've known for years, though I have seen less of him lately. He has a wife and a child now. As for colleagues, no. I have found it easier to work alone.'

'So you have no one?'

He frowned. 'In what way?'

'Someone to talk to. Someone to spend time with.'

'I have lovers whom I talk to. We have conversation over dinner, which is why I prefer an intelligent woman.'

Her heart squeezed tight. Not only was it clear he didn't have anyone, he didn't even know what she meant by that.

'I mean someone who knows you,' she said. 'Some-one who understands you. Someone you trust. Some-one you care for. Someone you can be intimate with.'

His features hardened and his gaze shuttered. 'No,' he said tersely. 'I do not. Nor do I need anyone like that.'

'Everyone needs someone like that.'

He abruptly lifted his wine and took a long swal-low before putting the glass back down with a thump. 'I don't.'

'You had no one? Not one person?'

'No,' he said flatly. 'After my mother left and I went into foster care, people weren't interested in making connections with me. Which was fine. I was happier in my own head.'

She didn't think it was fine, though. There was an insistence in his voice that sounded as if he was trying to convince himself as well as her. 'What about friends at school?' she persisted.

'School was boring, the other children dull. They didn't like me anyway, and I didn't like them.'

An uncompromising man. Then again, she already knew that too.

She studied him, the hard lines of his beautiful face, the steely glitter of his eyes.

For a time she'd tried to turn herself into a child she'd thought her aunt and uncle would notice, such as being like her cousins. She'd dyed her hair blonde, taken up hockey. But it hadn't worked, and it wasn't until after she'd left Perth that she'd realised that she needn't have bothered. Being like her cousins wouldn't have helped, because she was still *her*. She was still the girl that had been dumped on them and nothing would ever change that.

But Aristophanes hadn't bothered to change himself to suit anyone. He'd remained steadfastly who he was, resisting any effort to make himself more palatable to anyone.

It had made him lonely, yes, but he was splendid in his isolation.

She admired him for it.

'That must have been hard,' she said.

'It was not,' he said. 'As I said, I survived.'

'Survival isn't living, Bear.'

He scowled. 'What are you trying to say?'

'Nothing,' she said without heat. 'I'm only sad for you that you had such a rough childhood.'

'I wasn't beaten.' His voice was hard. 'I wasn't abused in any way. I had a roof over my head and I was fed. What more could have been done for me?'

'You could have been loved,' she said, not even knowing where the words had come from.

He stared at her a moment, the look in his eyes difficult to read. 'Love,' he echoed eventually, the word tinged with bitterness. 'Love left me sitting alone in a church at eight years old after my mother abandoned me. I didn't need love. I was better off without it.'

Her heart squeezed even tighter. It hurt to think about him as a lonely little boy. A boy who'd decided that love was just another word for abandonment, and who could blame him? He had reason. No one had ever given him the love he'd deserved, and he had deserved it. All children did. At least her memories of love had been good ones, happy ones. Even if she'd lost it and never found it again.

'I don't think you were,' she said gently. 'And your children definitely won't be.'

A muscle flicked at the side of his strong jaw. 'Are you saying that I won't love them?'

'No. I only mean that all children need love.'

'And so I will,' he said flatly. 'Don't worry about them.'

'I'm not worried about them. I'm worried about you.'

'Don't worry about me.' He stared at her across the table. 'This topic of conversation is uninteresting, so let's leave it. What are your plans for the future? Have you thought about it?'

She didn't want to drop the subject, but it was clear she wasn't going to get anything further from him, so she let it go.

'The future? Uh…no. No, I haven't.' She really hadn't. She'd been too busy thinking about how she was going to get through the next five months trapped on this island, let alone what would happen when the babies were born.

'Well, I have,' Aristophanes said, picking up his wine again and taking another swallow. 'I think that we should get married.'

A pulse of shock went through her. 'What?'

'It's a logical step. The twins will need both parents and we're agreed on that, so why not make it official? Marrying me will give you some security and legal protection should anything happen to me, and it will give our children a family.'

He said the words with such dispassion, as if he was talking about a business arrangement. Which was perhaps what marriage meant to him. Certainly, from what he'd said about love, he wasn't asking her because he was in love with her.

*This was what you wanted, though. You wanted a family.*

She always had. But she'd thought it would involve finding a man she loved and who loved her, not after an accidental night of passion, and certainly not with a man who found the idea of love abhorrent.

*He's not wrong, though. It will give you some secu-*

*rity. And after the children are born, you will also have physical passion...*

She took a breath. 'What about you? What will you get out of it?'

The flickering candlelight reflected the silver flames in his eyes. 'I will get a wife I very much want to spend time in bed with. Also, I will no longer need to schedule lovers to take care of my sexual needs so that will free up time to spend with the children.'

So. Sex and his damn schedule were all he cared about. She'd give him a couple of points for wanting to spend time with the children, but she had to deduct several million for being entirely blind to how it would affect her.

*And how exactly will it affect you? You want what he wants, and this will be good for the twins. This is about them, not you. What more is there?*

'I... I have to think about this,' she said uncertainly, her mind spinning.

'What is there to think about? You get my name, my money, and the children will be cared for. We will be a family.'

*A family...*

The words echoed through her. Yes, she wanted that. She wanted a family like the one she'd lost when her parents died. A family held together by love.

A sharp, painful feeling gathered in her gut.

She'd spent her whole childhood mourning, not only the loss of her parents, but the loss of the love they'd had for her, leaving a void inside her that had never been filled by her aunt and uncle.

*He won't fill it either, not now you know what he feels about love.*

'It's just…' She paused, her throat tightening. 'It's not only children who need love.' She steeled herself and looked at him. 'I do too.'

Across the table, Aristophanes' beautiful face remained hard. 'You do?' he demanded.

'My mum and dad loved me,' she said, her certainty gathering more and more weight with each second that passed. 'I knew that before they died. And the day they died, I lost that love. I spent my entire childhood mourning that loss, and swore to myself I'd find it again. Find myself someone who loved me the way I loved them. So… Yes. That's what I want in my future, Bear. I want a family. I want to love someone and I want them to love me, too.'

Steel glinted in his eyes. 'And you will have that. The children will love you.'

'The purpose of children isn't so they can love you. The purpose of children is to have their own lives.'

He scowled, which she was starting to think meant he didn't understand what she was talking about. 'Does it matter what source the love comes from?'

'Of course it does.' She felt tired all of a sudden, her appetite gone, her patience with him running thin. 'But I guess if you don't know what I'm talking about, then this is a pointless conversation.'

'Then explain it to me,' he insisted.

But Nell's energy had run out, and she didn't know why she was arguing with him anyway. After all, it couldn't be that she wanted love from him, it just couldn't. He was as in touch with his emotion as a rock and equally articulate, and she didn't want anything from him.

'No,' she said, putting down her lemonade glass. 'You know what? I'm tired and I can't be bothered, especially when you don't even have the slightest idea what I'm talking about.'

He gave her a ferocious look. 'Nell. Sit down.'

She ignored him, shoving her chair back and getting to her feet. 'Goodnight, Mr Katsaros,' she said.

'Nell!' he called after her as she strode towards the doorway to the salon. 'Sit down and explain!'

But she didn't.

She walked through the doors and back into the villa.

# CHAPTER NINE

ARISTOPHANES SAT IN his Athens office, scowling at the schedule on his computer screen. His schedule. He'd thought he'd set aside ample time to help Nell settle in—an afternoon and an evening was plenty. Or so he'd thought. But given their conversation the previous night, he was now starting to wonder.

He couldn't believe she'd walked away from him the night before. He'd only asked a question, wanting her to explain what she meant about love, and she'd just… walked away. It incensed him. Didn't she know how rare it was for him to need something explained? Didn't it matter to her? He'd have thought she'd jump at the chance, but no, she'd only looked tired and told him she 'couldn't be bothered'.

Unacceptable.

*Perhaps she was genuinely tired? She's pregnant with twins, remember?*

That was true. Possibly he needed to be more understanding. Still, he was trying. He wanted to give her what she needed for her well-being and for that of the twins, yet this love business mystified him.

Most people were in love when they got married, he knew that, but some weren't. For some it was an arrangement for legal purposes, which was what he'd been thinking when he'd asked her. He'd wanted some certainty for the future, and naturally legal protection and security for her, and he'd thought she'd see the logic behind the offer. But no, apparently not.

If he took into account her childhood and how miserable it had been, then he could almost see why it was important for her to feel loved. The difficulty for him, though, was that he didn't love her. He wasn't sure if it was even possible for him to feel love. He was certain he'd love his children—apparently that happened automatically the moment they were born—so he wasn't worried about that. It was she who concerned him.

He wanted her to say yes to his marriage offer. In fact, the more he thought about it, the more imperative it was that she accept. It would make things much simpler in the long run if she was his wife. He'd never have to bother with finding and scheduling lovers again, not with Nell in his bed, because their chemistry was still hot and strong. And she'd have the advantage of having his name. She'd never have to work again if she didn't want to, and if she did? Well, he'd create a school for her and she could run the place. Why not? The possibilities were endless.

Except if she didn't accept his offer, there would be no possibilities at all.

The tension in his gut twisted and he bared his teeth in a soundless growl.

No, he couldn't allow it. He had to get her to accept somehow and if that meant asking for some advice, then he'd ask for some damn advice.

Pulling his phone from his pocket, Aristophanes called Cesare.

'Another phone call?' Cesare said the minute he answered. 'And the second within two days of the first. Astonishing. Have you turned over a new leaf, Ari?'

Aristophanes glared out of the window and across the cluttered streets of Athens' downtown area. 'I need advice,' he said flatly.

'Intriguing. About your impending twins?'

'No, I'm sure that won't be an issue.' Aristophanes ignored his friend's slightly strangled laugh since there didn't seem to be anything amusing about what he'd said. 'It's about Nell. I have offered to marry her but… she refused.'

'I see.' Cesare's voice was suspiciously expressionless. 'How could that be? You're rich as Midas, have your health and all your own teeth. Not to mention a full head of hair. What more could she want?'

'I don't know,' Aristophanes replied, irritated. He *hated* not knowing something. 'I offered because we needed some certainty for the future. I thought it would also give her legal protection, not to mention creating a family for us. It's the next logical step.'

'Logical, hmm? That sounds like you. And speaking of, is this something you actually want? A wife, I mean.'

'Of course I want a wife. I wouldn't have asked her to marry me otherwise.'

'It's just that you've never professed any interest in wives.'

'I'm going to be a father, Cesare,' he said curtly. 'And you married Lark when you discovered she'd had your child.'

'True,' his friend admitted. 'Though it did take some time to learn how to be a proper husband and father.'

'I'm sure it will not be a problem for me,' Aristophanes said, because he was sure it wouldn't be. Again, if Cesare could do it, so could he. 'I only need her to accept my proposal.'

'Did she give you a reason for refusing you?'

Aristophanes was conscious of the ache in his jaw, a tight feeling running across his shoulders. 'She wants to be loved,' he said tightly.

Cesare sighed. 'Of course, she does. So I suppose this means you're not actually in love with her.'

'No.'

'And I suppose she's not actually Satan incarnate and thus completely unlovable?'

'Of course not,' he growled, bristling with defensiveness. 'She's the most beautiful woman I've ever met. She's intelligent, honest, stubborn, passionate and—'

'Yes, yes,' Cesare muttered. 'I get the idea. Are you sure you're not in love with her?'

'I'm not' he said, irritation becoming annoyance since this wasn't about him. It was about her. 'It isn't me we're talking about, Cesare.'

'Fine, fine. So she wants to be loved.'

'Yes. I told her that our children will love her, but

apparently it wasn't enough.' He picked up a pen and toyed restlessly with it. 'I wanted her to explain what kind of love she wanted, but she refused and told me she "couldn't be bothered".'

'Hmm,' Cesare said. 'Difficult.'

'Yes. And now I am at a loss. I want to change her mind, I want her to marry me, except I don't know how to do it.'

'I see. Well, you're the genius, Ari. Why don't you work it out?'

'I have,' he snapped. 'If we could sleep together, it would be fine. I would just seduce her into taking my ring. But sex is forbidden until the babies are born.'

Cesare was silent a long moment and Aristophanes fiddled incessantly with the pen, impatience and frustration winding tight inside him.

'You need to spend time with her,' Cesare said at length. 'Do some nice things for her. If you're not in love with her, the least you can do is make her feel as if you are.'

'Is that what you did for Lark?'

'Yes. I spent time with her and our little one, took them all around Italy. Showed her some of my favourite haunts. Wandered around eating gelato, that kind of thing.' His voice warmed. 'It was wonderful, and she loved it.'

There were obviously happy memories there for Cesare, so Aristophanes tried to think about similar things he could do with Nell and failed. He didn't have any favourite haunts. He didn't like gelato. His life consisted of flying from office to office, playing around with numbers and attending the odd gala when he absolutely had to. Which was not, he suspected, what Cesare was talking about.

'I don't know…what she would like,' he said at last.

'Then, my friend, may I suggest you find out? Perhaps even have a conversation or two?'

'I could just insist,' Aristophanes muttered, even more aggravated. 'Make her do what I said.'

'Tell me, my genius friend, have you *ever* tried making a woman do something she doesn't want to do?' Cesare asked. 'Not something I would recommend, not if you value any part of your manhood. And seriously, that would *not* be good for her well-being.'

Aristophanes threw the pen down on his desk in a snit. 'Do you, in fact, have any suggestions? Or are you just wasting my time?'

'You called me, remember?' Cesare said calmly. 'Good God, man. It's like you've never seduced a woman before.'

'I told you. We can't have sex—'

'I'm not talking about sex. Look, a woman isn't an equation to be solved or an algorithm to compute. She's a person. A human being. Find out what she likes to do, what her interests are. Listen to her. Remember, Ari, sometimes the most important gift you can give to a person is your time.'

Time. A precious commodity and that he understood. But did Nell even want his time? He'd told her about his

schedule, about its importance, but would she understand if he gave her some of that?

*Why does it matter that she understands you? This
is about her, remember?*

The thought sat in his head after he'd ended the call,
and he found himself sitting and staring out of the window once again, his mind working feverishly. Thinking about Nell. Thinking about her childhood, about
her aunt and uncle. About how she'd been made to feel
as if her existence was something that went unnoticed
and unappreciated.

Nell had survived without love, it was true, as he
had. But she'd also said that surviving wasn't living.
And while he didn't quite understand what she meant
by that, he did understand that she'd had love once, before her parents had died. For her, love had been a good
thing and she'd mourned its loss.

He couldn't remember what love had been like for
him. Perhaps the vague recollection of his mother's em-
brace. A kiss on the head. A smile. Yet every one of
those things had been negated by what had followed it.
Sitting in an emptying church pew, waiting, waiting.
The gradual realisation that his mother wasn't coming to
get him. The sense of a dark pit opening up inside him,
a pit he was going to fall headlong into. Because she'd
left him there. She'd left him there alone, unwanted—

He jerked his thoughts away. Again, this wasn't about
him. This was about Nell. He didn't love her, but perhaps
he could make her feel as if he did. Give her the things
she'd missed out on in her life: attention and care and

respect. Easy enough to do in bed, naturally, but he was going to have to think of different ways to do it now.

The thought galvanised him. He'd always loved a challenge and he had a couple of ideas already spinning in his head, so he leaned forward to his computer and, with a couple of mouse clicks, cleared his entire schedule for the next week.

Then he began planning.

Nell sat by the pool, on a lounger, trying to pay attention to the book she'd found in the villa's library, and failing. It was annoying that she felt just as miserable now as she had when she'd gone to bed the night before, hoping a good sleep would help. Except she hadn't had a good sleep. After leaving Aristophanes and the lovely dinner he'd laid out for her the night before, she'd gone to her bedroom and lain down, hoping oblivion would come. Instead, she'd tossed and turned, her head full of him and his marriage offer.

She shouldn't have walked away from him. She should have stayed and tried to explain what she wanted, because it was clear he didn't know, and that wasn't his fault.

It wasn't as if he'd had a normal childhood. He'd been abandoned by the one person who was supposed to love him, then gone from foster family to foster family, making no connections with anyone. Withdrawing into himself deeper and deeper, escaping into that wonderful mind of his.

A lonely man. A man who had no idea about love.

And while he might be a genius with numbers and money, he was functionally illiterate when it came to emotions.

Last night it had all felt too much and she didn't even know why she was staying here. She wasn't a prisoner after all and, while he was offering a great deal of support for their children, it was obvious he didn't care that much for her.

She didn't know why she wanted him to, either.

Nell pulled the brim of the hat she was wearing down lower, so it shaded her nose from the hot Greek sun, and stared so hard at her book the print blurred.

Sex had blinded her, that was the issue. She'd been rendered so breathless by his touch and the way he made her feel physically that she'd expected the same feeling to follow on naturally out of bed as in it. And it hadn't. Their interactions were fraught and stilted when sex was taken out of the equation, and she didn't know how to make it better.

*Yet you reached for his hand that night in Melbourne. And you reached for it again that day in New York when you thought you might lose the babies. And he took it. He held you as tightly as you held him.*

This was true. As if something deep inside her, something wordless and instinctive, automatically reached for him in times of trouble, and found him.

She didn't understand it. Words were supposed to aid communication and yet with her and Aristophanes, they got in the way. They communicated far better in bed than they ever did out of it, but sadly a marriage was about more than sex.

Nell let out a breath, finally giving up reading and watching the sun glint off the water of the pool.

*Would it really be so bad being married to him? You'd be looked after financially and that would mean great security for the twins. You'd have all the passion you could stand once the babies are born too. You could insist on a career, he wouldn't deny you that, and you could even have your own life apart from his.*

All of that was true and all of it was attractive. Plus he hadn't been wrong when he'd said the children would love her. She'd have them, at least. Then again, she didn't want to put that kind of pressure on them. They didn't exist to fulfil her need for love. They existed for their own sake and she would love them. This was all, after all, for them.

Still, she wanted a marriage to exist for its own sake too. Not for legal reasons or because she was pregnant. She'd wanted the kind of family she'd lost, the kind of marriage her parents had. She'd been only a child when they'd died, so she'd had no idea what their relationship had been like, but she did remember her mother kissing her father. Her father holding her mother. They'd been happy together, she was sure.

Was it so wrong to want that for herself? After years of being resented for her mere existence?

'Nell.'

The deep, masculine voice cut through her thoughts, and she jerked her head up, her heartbeat going into overdrive as Aristophanes' tall figure stepped out of the French doors and into the pool area, striding over to her sun lounger with his usual animal grace.

She pushed her hat back on her head and looked up at him.

He stood beside the lounger, tall and dark, the sun outlining his powerful figure like streams of glory around a god.

*You might be in trouble here...*

'What are you doing back?' she asked, ignoring both the thought and the husk in her voice. 'I thought you were in Athens all week.'

'I was.' His eyes had taken on a familiar silver glitter, making her heartbeat even faster. 'But I have decided something. I have a gala in London I have to attend, and I wondered if you would like to come with me. I thought we could visit my good friend Cesare in Rome first, then go on to London. Perhaps we could do some sightseeing, if you are up to it.'

A little shock washed through her. He wanted her company? And to introduce her to his friend? That was definitely not about the pregnancy. 'Go with you?' she said, a little uncertainly. 'But I thought I was supposed to stay here. Be on bed rest.'

'You are not limited to lying in bed, and, in fact, some exercise is good for you. The doctor will accompany us to London.' He paused a moment, as if thinking something over. Then he went on, a little haltingly. 'I...don't wish to go to the gala. I get impatient with social functions and don't enjoy them. However, it's important for me to attend and so I would like…your company. We need only stay for a short time.'

Something in the region of her heart tightened. 'But… why?' she couldn't help asking. 'I mean, why do you want me there?'

Aristophanes' gaze abruptly became focused and intense, making her breath catch. 'Because you are beautiful and you are better with people than I am. I want you on my arm, dazzling everyone in a pretty gown and fine jewels, with your lovely smile. I want the entire world to know that this amazing woman is mine and no one else can have her.'

Her heart tightened even more, heat stealing through her cheeks at his praise, a bone-deep longing clutching inside her. To be on his arm in a wonderful gown, the centre of attention at an important party, in London. To be his…

'Is that what I am?' she couldn't help asking. 'Yours?'

'Yes,' he said without hesitation, an edge of finality in his voice that should have annoyed her, because she was no one's, surely. Yet she wasn't annoyed. For some reason it reassured her in a way she wasn't expecting. 'There will be media there,' he went on. 'And no doubt there'll be some speculation about who you are, but I want everyone to be in no doubt that you're mine. However, if you're concerned for your and the twins' privacy, I can make sure it is protected.'

She swallowed. 'So…how am I yours? Am I your girlfriend?'

Again, silver flickered in his gaze. 'What do you

want to be? I would prefer you to be my fiancée, but I understand why you can't.'

'Do you?' she asked, searching the hard lines of his face. 'Do you really understand?'

Aristophanes stared down at her, quiet for a long moment. 'You want to be loved, Nell,' he said at last. 'And yes, I understand why. At least, I think I do. You want what you lost when your parents died, what you never had from your aunt and uncle. And I have to be honest, but I can't give that to you. I think when my mother left me, something inside me broke, something that can't be repaired.'

The tightness in her chest gathered into pain. 'Oh, Bear, I can't—'

'Hush,' he interrupted softly. 'I haven't finished. I want to say that while I can't give you what you want, I think I can make you feel as if you had it. I think I can make you happy.' A muscle in his jaw leapt. 'I'd like to try, if you'll let me.' His expression was intent, the full focus of his considerable attention turned on her, making her feel breathless. Making her feel as if she were the only person worth looking at in the entire world.

But it hurt too. Because perhaps it was true what he'd said, that he was broken. That when he'd been abandoned, a vital part of him had shattered, never to be repaired, and he certainly gave every impression of a man who'd had some vital emotional connection severed.

Yet, he wanted this; she could see it in his eyes. It was important to him; it meant something to him. *She* meant something to him.

She didn't want to be a woman drawn to men in need of fixing. She'd really rather the man came fixed already. Yet she was in deep now, perhaps too deep. She'd seen his loneliness, even if he didn't know the depths of it himself, and because she too was lonely, she knew how it felt. She knew how it hurt, and she didn't want that for him.

That was why it was too late to leave him, she realised with sudden insight. That was why she hadn't left the island already. Not only because of the lack of support and her anxieties about her pregnancy, but because of him.

And maybe he wasn't broken, maybe he'd only been wounded. Which meant she didn't need to fix him, but to heal him, and that was a different thing, that was something she could do. He obviously needed more than a kiss on the head and a sticking plaster, which was what she did for the kids she taught when they hurt themselves, but she could try. Perhaps even, in healing him, she'd find a measure of healing for herself too, such as being on his arm, in a beautiful dress, at an important party in London.

Perhaps he was even right that feeling loved was all she needed. It didn't have to be real in order for her to be happy, and, if nothing else, at least she'd get a trip to London. So, she might as well go with him. What else did she have to lose?

Nell stared up at him, drawing out the moment shamelessly, because it wouldn't do him any harm to wait a little for her answer, maybe even suffer a little. Then she eased herself out of the sun lounger and got to her feet, only inches between them. He smelled so good, making her breath catch and the hungry place between her thighs ache.

'Nell,' he murmured, soft and gravelly, the silver flames in his eyes leaping high. 'You should not get so close to me. Especially when you're only wearing a bikini.'

'But if I'm going to be on your arm,' she said, looking up at him from beneath her lashes, 'we're going to need to practise being close to each other, aren't we?'

He smiled then, quick and blinding, the charm of it stealing her breath clean away, and perhaps taking her heart along with it.

Then it was gone, his features reverting to a slightly less tense version of his usual stony expression. 'Good,' he said. 'I'll have the staff pack for you. We'll leave for Rome tonight. I'll show you the schedule I have planned on the plane.'

# CHAPTER TEN

ARISTOPHANES SAT ON the terrace of Cesare's villa in Rome and watched as Cesare's daughter, Maya, ran over to where Nell was sitting at the other end of the long table with Lark. They'd been at Cesare and Lark's for a couple of nights on their way to London, and Aristophanes had felt a burst of possessive pride at how much both Cesare and his wife liked Nell, as did their daughter.

Now the little girl leaned against Nell as she showed Nell the picture she'd drawn. Automatically Nell had put her arm around her as she asked Maya questions about the picture, listening intently as Maya explained.

He could see why Nell was so good with children. She gave Maya all her attention and was endlessly patient with the little girl's chatter.

Cesare was talking to him about something, but Aristophanes wasn't listening. All he could see was Nell, imagining her with their own son and daughter, talking to them about the pictures they'd drawn or playing with them, or even just holding them. It made his chest tighten, made him feel possessive, hungry almost, wanting things he couldn't articulate.

Just then, Nell looked over at him and smiled before whispering something in the little girl's ear. Maya instantly picked up her drawing and ran over to where Aristophanes sat, clambering up onto his knee without any apparent shyness and demanding he look at her picture.

Nell leaned on the table, her chin in her hand, watching him with a kind of gentle amusement that held such warmth that for a moment he couldn't breathe. And he had the strangest sense that he knew exactly what she was thinking, and it was the same thing he was, about their children and what it would be like to have this. Them, together, with their son and daughter.

He smiled at her, he couldn't help it, and his heart clenched when she smiled back in a perfect moment of understanding.

*How* can *you understand, though? When you don't know what love is?*

The thought was an ugly one, so he ignored it, and concentrated on Maya and looking at her drawing instead.

That perfect moment of understanding he'd experienced, however, lingered, the warmth of it colouring the rest of their visit with Cesare and Lark, and it was still there a week later, when Aristophanes had the limo pull up outside the sweeping stone steps of the deconsecrated church that had been turned into a five-star event space. The gala—a charity fundraiser—was being held there and already a sizeable crowd of onlookers and paparazzi had built up around the entrance.

It was going to be an exclusive event and Cesare had informed him that it was one of the highlights of London's social calendar and thus well attended, which satisfied him immensely. He wanted the crowd to be large and the event important, so he could present Nell to as many people as possible. As he'd told her back in Greece, he wanted the world to see what a beautiful woman he'd managed to snare.

Now he stared out through the limo window, noting the press standing by the stairs, and feeling that same deep sense of satisfaction, plus an anticipatory thrill that he never experienced when going to social engagements.

It was her, of course. Tonight she would be on his arm, and for the first time in his life he found himself actually looking forward to getting out of the limo and walking up those stairs, to entering the venue, and having people notice him. Having them notice her.

Looking forward to showing her around and showing her off. Introducing her to people and having them be charmed by her instead of having to make awkward conversation with him. They would be captivated by her and how could they not? Especially when he was.

Completely and utterly.

He felt her hand rest briefly on his thigh and he turned to look at her, sitting beside him in the limo.

Good God, she was lovely.

He'd had gowns brought to his London residence in Knightsbridge for her to try on, and they'd all without exception been spectacular. But the one she'd eventually chosen was truly remarkable, of deep red silk that he'd thought would clash with her hair, yet somehow didn't. The gown had little sleeves that dropped slightly off her shoulders while the bodice gently cupped her lovely breasts, the skirts flowing down gracefully over her little bump.

Her hair had been gathered on top of her head, with one long lock curling around her neck and falling down to graze the rise of her breasts, and she wore the simple waterfall necklace of glittering rubies that he'd bought for her.

She looked beautiful. Exquisite. And so luscious he wanted to take a bite out of her.

'You really don't like these things, do you?' she asked quietly, a crease between her brows as she studied him. 'Why not?'

He didn't know how she managed to always know what he was feeling. It was as if she had some kind of inbuilt radar automatically attuned to him, and he should have found it as annoying as he had a couple of weeks earlier, when she'd first come to him in New York with news of her pregnancy. But for some reason, he didn't now. He had, after all, given her a little piece of himself back in Greece, when he'd first revealed his London plans to her, revealing that he didn't like social engagements.

*You didn't have to tell her you were broken, though.*

No, he didn't. But he hadn't been able to lie to her, tell her he could give her something that he couldn't. She had to know that there was a part of him that didn't work properly, that couldn't be fixed. It wasn't fair otherwise.

He put his hand over hers where it rested on his thigh, the warmth of her skin a comfort he hadn't anticipated. 'I find them a waste of time. Small talk is pointless and no one wants to talk about anything of any value.'

She smiled. 'You must be fun at parties.'

'I don't like parties,' he said.

Her dark eyes sparkled. 'I'm teasing you, Bear.'

He couldn't think when she smiled at him that way. There were literally no thoughts in his head right now except how velvety and soft her eyes looked, and how biteable her mouth was, and how silky her skin seemed. How her smile made him want to check the sky through the window to see if the sun had somehow come out, even though it was night.

And a sudden realisation caught at him in an intense, breath-stealing rush: he couldn't let her go after this. Not after they got back to Greece, and definitely not after their twins were born. He couldn't let her go. Not ever.

He wanted to tell her, right here, right now, that she wasn't ever to leave him, that she couldn't, but he bit down hard on the words. Not now. Later, after the gala, he'd tell her. When they had some privacy enough that he could convince her to take his ring. He'd tell her anything she wanted to hear if it meant she'd agree to be his wife.

They couldn't stay long here anyway, not given her condition. The doctor had okayed the event, but told him that Nell could stay only a couple of hours at most, and that she wasn't to be on her feet the whole time.

So he didn't speak and instead gripped her hand, and when the driver opened the limo door, he got out first, then helped her from the car and into the glare of the paparazzi's cameras.

She was smiling as she stared around, gripping tight to his hand, and the paparazzi began calling his name and taking pictures. Wanting to know who she was and what she was wearing, all the usual things.

Strangely, he found himself smiling too, watching her excitement at all the fuss.

'Do I tell them who I am?' she asked as they walked up the stairs hand in hand.

'Do you want to?' he murmured back. 'Or would you rather be my mystery woman?' He'd thought she might prefer that, but he hadn't been sure. Yet her mischievous smile confirmed that he'd been right, which made him feel extremely pleased with himself.

'Definitely your mystery woman,' she said, and gave him a look from beneath her lashes that nearly incinerated him with desire on the spot. He didn't know how he was going to last the next few months of her pregnancy without touching her. It would likely kill him.

But while not touching her was a torture, the gala itself turned out to be the best he'd ever attended in his entire life. It had nothing to do with the venue or the occasion, and everything to do with Nell.

Nell's hand in his and her excitement as they went inside and she kept pointing out celebrities, politicians, and the odd royal. Then her asking questions about who the other people were—CEOs like himself and other industry leaders—and so he spent a good deal of time telling her who they were and explaining what industries they were in.

Nell, and how she glittered as brightly as her ruby necklace, catching fire from the auburn glints in her hair and the deep red of her mouth.

Nell, and how she somehow managed to make the conversation with people flow so easily and so naturally, it made him wonder why he'd ever found it so difficult.

Nell, who made him find out what charity this was in aid of and then, when he discovered it was a children's charity, wanted to be introduced to the CEO and then had a long discussion with them about children in need.

He stood by her side, watching her, unable to take his eyes off her. Listening to her talk confidently about kids and what they needed, and how important it was to the future of society to look after the children of today.

It mystified him how he could ever have thought that she was somehow less intelligent than any of his dates. Bewildered him how he could ever have looked down on her choice of career. Puzzled him how he'd managed to get this far in life without her in it.

Because if she wasn't in it, he didn't know if he could survive.

*That's why you have to hold onto her. She can't leave you. She can't ever leave you, yet you know she might. After all, your mother left you...*

Ice wound through him, turning his fingertips numb.

No, that thought was wrong. Nell wouldn't leave him. How could she? He was the father of her children; she had to stay with him. She didn't have the support she needed at home and, also, she was happy; he was certain of it.

There was no way she could leave. He wouldn't allow it. He'd just keep on making her so happy she'd never leave him.

Yet no matter what he told himself, the icy feeling in his gut wouldn't go away.

A reminder on his watch went off, letting him know it was time for Nell to sit down again, so, gripping her elbow and murmuring a few excuses, he steered her away from the charity CEO and over to a comfortable-looking couch placed in a nook by a pillar.

'This is getting tiresome,' she said as she sat down. 'I was enjoying that conversation.'

'I know. But you will have plenty more opportunities to talk once the babies are born.' He sat down next to her, keeping her hand in his, not wanting to release it. 'We should probably go. You need rest.'

'I'm fine.' She squeezed his hand reassuringly. 'How are you?'

'Tonight's occasion has been surprisingly bearable,' he said, trying to force down the strange pressure that had been building in his chest. 'You will have to come with me whenever I'm invited to these interminable things.'

She smiled and the pressure increased, making his heart feel full of air, inflating hard against his ribs. 'Of course. Just buy me another pretty dress and a gorgeous necklace like this one, and I'll go wherever you ask.'

She was teasing him, making him feel as if living weren't quite as heavy as it was. As if there were something light to be found in it, something joyful.

Happiness. Was this what she meant when she said she wanted to be happy? This effervescent feeling, as if he were full of champagne bubbles, all rising and bursting and rising again. It made him want to keep this moment, lock it in amber somehow, her dark eyes full of warmth and tender amusement, her mouth curving in the most beautiful smile and all for him.

*Your mother smiled at you, too, remember? Just before she walked away.*

Ice pierced him and his fingers around hers tightened. 'You can't leave, Nell,' he said far too abruptly, the ice closing around his throat. 'You can never leave.'

A brief look of shock flickered through her eyes. 'What do you mean never leave?'

'You can never leave me.' He held onto her hand even tighter, feeling all at once as if he would drown if he let her go. 'You can't. I won't let you.'

She stared at him, her smile fading, the excitement vanishing.

*This is what you will do to her. What you do to everyone. It's no mystery why your mother walked away. You lack something fundamental that makes anyone want to stay.*

His heartbeat in his head sounded like a funeral march.

'Bear?' She looked concerned now. 'What's wrong? Why are you talking like this?'

He'd make her smile fade, make her go pale. He'd keep her on the island, imprison her so she'd never leave, yet in doing so, he'd suffocate her.

He would keep her from what she wanted most.

Love.

Pain knifed through him all of a sudden as another thought came to him.

The babies, his children. His son and his daughter. He'd thought loving them would be automatic, but what if it wasn't? Cesare loved his daughter, but then Cesare loved his wife too. What if Aristophanes couldn't? What if he couldn't love his children? He remembered that moment the week before, at Cesare's villa, when he'd met Nell's gaze and known that they'd both been thinking about how they would be together as a family. But...what if he couldn't do that? If he couldn't love Nell, how could he love them?

Nell raised her free hand and laid her palm against his cheek. 'Bear?'

It took everything he had, but he managed it, opening his hand and letting her fingers slide from his. Then he took her palm from his cheek and laid it back down on the red silk of her lap.

'You were right,' he said roughly. 'You were right all this time.'

'Right?' Not even a ghost of a smile turned her mouth now. 'Right about what? What's going on, Aristophanes? You're scaring me.'

He'd never hated his name more than he did in that moment. 'You do deserve to be loved, Nell. You deserve to have the family you lost, and you deserve happiness. You deserve much more than anything I can give you.'

Her eyes went wide, as if he'd slapped her. 'What are you talking about?'

'I can't give you the love you want.'

'I know, you told me—'

'And I don't think I ever will,' he said, cutting her off. 'I told you: I'm missing something…inside me. Something important. Something vital.'

'You're not missing anything.' The rubies of her necklace glittered in time with her quickened breath, her dark eyes searching his face. 'You're just hurt. Wounded.'

He shook his head hard. 'No. It's not a wound, Nell. It was already there. It had to be. Why else would my mother have walked away?'

'You can't know—'

'I can't love you, Nell. I don't know how. I don't know if I can even love our children, and I can't—*won't*—allow that possibility.' He took a breath and steeled himself because he knew what he had to do now. The only thing he could think of that would save her. 'You have to leave me, understand? You have to walk away from me and never look back.'

Shock, cold as ice, seeped through her as she stared into his eyes.

He was so certain. She could see that. He believed it totally. That there was something missing from him, something broken. He'd told her as much back in Greece, and it had hurt her then. It hurt even more now. More than she'd ever thought possible.

'You're wrong,' she said in a tight voice, emotion almost strangling her. 'I don't know why your mother walked away, but it was the worst thing in the world a mother can do to their child. You were eight years old and there was nothing wrong with you.'

'The other foster families—'

'You were traumatised,' she interrupted, reaching for his hand again. 'You were abandoned by your mother, then shipped to live with complete strangers. You were bounced from one to another, and no one made an effort with you. No one bothered to connect with you. But that's a trauma, Bear. That's a wound. It doesn't mean you're broken.'

But he was shaking his head, removing his hand from hers yet again, because she was wrong. 'I wasn't wounded when she left me in that church,' he said roughly. 'I was whole then. Or at least, I thought I was. Logic suggests otherwise.'

It felt as if he'd reached inside her and it wasn't her hand he was squeezing now, but her heart. Making it ache. Making it hurt. 'You can't think these things,' she said desperately. 'You can't ever know why—'

'No.' The word was a growl. 'I can't do it. I can't risk it. Something dark in me wants nothing more than to keep you and the twins, and it will do anything in its power to make sure you can never leave. But I can't do that to you, Nell. There will never be happiness for you if that happens.'

She swallowed, her throat thick, her chest aching at the desperation she saw in his eyes. 'You don't even want to try?'

'I could, but what if it doesn't work? What if there *is* something wrong? What if the babies are born and I feel nothing for them? What would that do to them? What would that do to you?' He shifted suddenly, putting some distance between them. 'I thought I would love them automatically, but I could be wrong. Some people don't love their children, Nell.' His gaze had darkened, going from brilliant silver to tarnished steel. 'My mother didn't love me, did she? If she did, she wouldn't have walked away.'

Nell had never wanted to slap someone as hard as she wanted to slap the woman who'd left her little boy sitting alone in a church. Left him to be given to one family and then another, like an unwanted present. Was it any wonder he felt this way? With a childhood like his?

She ached and ached for him.

He was so beautiful in the black evening clothes he wore. Simple, exquisitely tailored, showing off his broad shoulders and narrow waist. His black hair, his silver eyes. His focused intensity, his electric presence.

He'd been at her side all night, holding her hand, and she'd felt him watch her, as if he hadn't been able to look at anyone else. So many celebrities and famous people here at this gala, and all he'd been interested in was her.

He'd bought her the most beautiful gown to wear and

the glorious necklace. Yet even without them, she'd still feel the way she had that first night together. Beautiful. Special. Like a treasure he'd uncovered and couldn't believe was his. Because it wasn't the gown or the jewels that made her feel that way. It was the glittering intensity in his eyes whenever he looked at her, the flickering heat, the desire. As if she was the only woman for him.

He'd cleared his schedule for her and she knew what that meant to him. He'd introduced her to his friend, Cesare, and his wonderful wife, Lark, and their adorable little girl. And she'd had a moment watching him as Maya had hauled herself into his lap, waving her drawing in his face, and the granite lines of his face had softened. Then he'd looked over at her and smiled, and she'd been able to see him all at once, with their own children, a patient, caring father.

He'd even handed her an organised itinerary of their visit to London, each part of the day set aside for different activities. It was very Aristophanes. But some blocks of time simply had 'Nell's choice' on them, which she'd been delighted by.

He'd made an effort, she understood. Made an effort to get to know her, to understand what she'd meant when she'd said she'd wanted to be loved. An effort to make her happy.

She still wanted those things. Yet she was also beginning to understand that it wasn't just any man she wanted those things from.

She wanted *him* to make her happy, because she wouldn't be happy with anyone else.

She wanted *him* to love her, because it didn't mean anything if it wasn't him.

No other man meant anything except him.

*You love him.*

Of course she did. Perhaps she'd loved him that moment she'd opened her eyes on the pavement in Melbourne, and found him leaning over her, her hand in his, the warmth and strength of him flowing into her.

He was aggravating, oblivious, arrogant, and wanted his own way far too much. But he was also caring, honest, protective, and, maybe even more than all of those, he wanted to understand.

This man wasn't broken. He was wounded. He'd put his emotions away in a box so they didn't hurt him any more and had carried on with his life as if they weren't there. But they were there, and now they were escaping the box and he didn't know what to do.

Her eyes filled with tears; she couldn't help it. Tears for him. For the little boy he'd once been, who'd been abandoned in a church. A church like the one they were sitting in right now. And for the man he'd become, armoured and closed off and yet, despite all of that, still caring. Still wanting a connection. Needing it. She could see the strength of that need in his eyes. Had felt it in his arms late at night too. He had love inside him, a whole ocean of it, but he couldn't access it, that was his problem. He didn't even know it was there.

'You can't let what your mother did define who you are,' she said. 'You're more than just a genius, Bear. You're kind and protective and caring. You have everything you need to be a wonderful father and I have no doubts at all that you will be.' Her throat ached. She could barely swallow. 'I don't want to walk away from you. In fact, I've changed my mind. I think I do want to marry you after all.'

The expression on his face lit with something so bright she could barely look at it, and then it vanished, gone as if it had never been. 'No. I can't allow it. I can't give you what you want, remember?'

'But what if I don't need it?' She blinked fiercely, not wanting to cry. 'What if me loving you is all I need?'

He stared at her. 'You love me?' he asked blankly.

There was no reason to deny it and she didn't want to. 'Yes. I think I loved you the moment I opened my eyes on that pavement in Melbourne and saw you leaning over me.'

'Nell—'

'It's enough. It's enough for both of us.' She reached for him a third time. 'Let's try. I want to.'

He'd gone very still, making no move towards her hand, the expression in his eyes one she couldn't interpret. Then abruptly, everything about him went dark, shadows in his eyes, across his face, his features hard as rock.

'No,' he said. 'There is no point in trying if you can't do it. And I can't do it.' He turned away from her, staring stonily ahead. 'Leave, please.'

She blinked. 'Bear, please—'

'*Leave,*' he said, with so much quiet emphasis he might have roared it.

Shaking in every part of her, Nell slowly got to her feet, looking down at the man she loved. And a sudden lash of anger caught at her. 'That's it,' she said. 'Make me be the one to walk away. Turn me into the bad guy, turn me into your mother. It's easier, isn't it, to order someone to leave you than ask them to stay?'

'You aren't the bad guy,' he said. 'I was the one who told you to go. It's better for you and for the babies. Better for all of us.'

'But you're not giving me a choice, Aristophanes. You're deciding for me.'

He turned then and looked up at her, his eyes nothing but dull grey iron. 'Now you know why I'm not the husband for you.'

'It's not better,' she said, trying one last time. 'It's not better for me or our babies if you're not there.'

'Yes, it is,' he said tonelessly.

She stood there for a moment, feeling as though her world were shattering slowly into pieces. 'For all that you're supposed to be a genius,' she whispered, 'you're actually a very, very stupid man.'

Then she turned and left him sitting there, on a bench in a church, alone.

# CHAPTER ELEVEN

ARISTOPHANES HAD NEVER found alcohol to be all that enlightening, but by the time he arrived back at his London residence that night, he'd decided that perhaps he needed to try it. Anything that might blunt the sharp edges of the pain in his chest, a pain that seemed to grow wider and deeper with every passing second.

He'd done the right thing, he was certain. It had been the hardest thing he'd ever done in his life to make her walk away from him, but he'd managed it. He'd taken himself out of the equation and now there was nothing in her way to prevent her from having the kind of life she deserved.

As to their children, well, he would have to deal with that at some point. They were probably better off without him. At least they'd have one parent who wasn't irretrievably damaged by their past.

On arrival at his residence, he was informed that Nell wasn't at home, which immediately alarmed him, at least until one of his staff informed him that she'd taken herself off to a hotel for the evening.

That made the pain inside him grow teeth, long and

sharp, and he sent a couple of staff off to check she was okay and to make sure she had everything she needed.

Really, it should have been him going to the hotel, not her. Then again, that was another reason why he would make her a terrible husband.

After that had been accomplished, he went into his study, shut the door, and conducted a very thorough investigation of a bottle of whisky, along with an experiment in how many glasses it would take to make the pain inside him go away.

When morning came around, he was none the wiser as to how many glasses since the pain was still there, eating away at him like rust in iron, and he was on the point of getting another bottle when the door of the study opened, and Cesare walked in.

Aristophanes, slumped in an armchair, scowled at him. 'What the hell are you doing here?' he demanded gracelessly.

'Apparently you're worrying people,' Cesare said, throwing himself into the armchair opposite, stretching his legs out and folding his hands comfortably on his flat stomach. 'People who shall remain nameless.'

Aristophanes didn't stop scowling. 'You're interrupting my drinking.'

'You do know you're expecting twins, right?'

'They are better off without me.' He lifted the bottle of Scotch and poured the last remaining drops into his tumbler.

Cesare lifted a dark brow. 'And who decided that?'

'I did.'

'So, you're already deciding things for your children.' He nodded. 'Spoken like a true father.'

Aristophanes, who'd never found his friend more irritating and his presence more pointless than he did right now, changed his scowl to a glare. 'You are mocking me.'

'You deserve to be mocked,' Cesare said unrepentantly. 'You're going to have twins and here you are, sitting in your study drinking and brooding like an eighteen-year-old. All the while, your lovely Nell is very upset and I'm not sure it's wise to leave her like that in her condition.'

His lovely Nell. Beautiful, wonderful Nell.

The pain reached epic proportions, but he shoved it away, and studied his glass of Scotch instead. It was distressingly almost empty. 'I am sparing her,' he said.

'And what exactly are you sparing her?'

'The pain of being with me.' He tossed back what little Scotch there was in the glass. 'You don't understand.'

Cesare shook his head. 'Of course, I don't understand. Me, who had no idea what to do with a surprise daughter and a woman who turned me inside out. Me, who now has the world's most wonderful wife and child, and who is now blissfully happy. No, I definitely don't understand anything about that.'

'It is not the same,' Aristophanes growled. 'You are able to love—'

'Everyone can love, you idiot,' Cesare growled right back. 'Unless you're a sociopath and I'm pretty certain you're not one of those. Also, I think you're already in love with her. The choice is whether you accept it or keep on being your usual grumpy self. Scheduling lovers when you have the time and scheduling father moments along with them. I'm sure you'll be happy doing that.'

Aristophanes gritted his teeth and stared at his friend. 'I am *not* in love with her.'

'Then why are you drinking?' Cesare's blue stare was uncompromising. 'Why did you send her away? And why are you looking at me as if you want to kill me?'

'Because you're annoying,' he said, meeting Cesare stare for stare. 'Make yourself useful and get me another bottle of Scotch.'

'No,' Cesare said tersely. 'Do you remember what you said to me when I was agonising about being enough for Lark?'

Aristophanes shifted in his chair, not wanting to think about it. 'I do not.'

'You said, and I quote, "You have a beautiful daughter and a lovely wife. Be a shame to throw all that away because you're not brave enough to man up."'

'It's not the same,' he began roughly. 'It's different—'

'It's not different,' Cesare interrupted. 'You were right. I did have to man up. And so do you. You say you can't love, but that's just an excuse. You're as capable of it as any man, but you're afraid. Because love is vulnerability. Love is pain. Love is wondering if you're ever going to be enough for someone but choosing to try anyway, because they're worth it. Because love is worth it.'

His chest ached, agony echoing inside him. Was his friend right? Was that pain love? Was that why his life, which had kept him content for so long, suddenly seemed bleak and worthless? Had it always been like that and he just hadn't seen it? And if so, why did he only see it now?

But, of course, he knew the answer to that, didn't he?

*You are afraid.*

The thought wound through his brain and his instinct was to shove it away, but now the words had been said, it was all he could think about. He'd told Nell he was broken, that love was impossible for him, but if that was true then why did he hurt so much? Why did he want to punch Cesare in the face for telling him he was afraid?

*Because it's true. Because it's easier to tell someone to leave than to ask them to stay.*

That was what Nell had said to him before he'd made her leave. And yes, he'd made her. She'd wanted to stay with him. She *loved* him.

Agony twisted inside him, and a suspicion began to grow. What if it was true? That the pain he felt now was actually love? And what if the fear that lay at the heart of him was love too? What if all the doubt and anger were also love?

'How?' he demanded suddenly into the tense silence. 'How are any of those things worth it?'

The look on Cesare's face softened slightly. 'That's just one side of the coin, Ari. There's the other side too. Which is knowing there's one person in the world who will be on your side no matter what, and who makes your life better just by existing. Who brings out the best in you. Who makes you happy. What's worth more than that?'

Aristophanes went very still as realisation came, slowly but very, very surely.

She made his life better just by existing. She made him happy. That was why his life felt bleak and meaningless now—because she wouldn't be in it. He'd sent her away.

*You gave her nothing but excuses. You're afraid that, because of your mother, you're not enough for a woman like her and you never will be. And you're in love with her and you have been ever since you saw her.*

And now he was hurting her.

*'It's not better for me or our babies if you're not there.'*

That was what she'd said to him the night before, and there had been tears in her eyes, pain too. She loved him, even though he'd told her he was broken, that he couldn't give her what she wanted. She loved him anyway. She loved him in spite of that. She thought being with him was worth all the terrible things on the other side of that coin.

She'd chosen love.

His beautiful Nell. Braver by far than he was, braver than he'd ever be. And she was right. He was a stupid man.

Of course love was worth all the terrible things it also brought with it, the pain and the doubt and awful vulnerability. Because that was not all love was. There was the pleasure and intimacy he found in her arms. The happiness that filled him when he made her smile. The delight of listening to her talk to people and charm them and make everything less fraught. The joy of watching her with Maya and knowing that soon she would be that way with their own children and how he couldn't wait to see it. The wordless comfort he felt when she reached for his hand and held it, knowing she was with him and that, together, they could face anything.

She made his life better in every conceivable way. How could that not be worth it?

Aristophanes clumsily put down his tumbler on the floor, feeling strangely light-headed as a powerful feeling swept through him, burning, intense, like liquid flame.

'Did she call you?' he asked. 'Did she ask you to come here?'

'She wanted me to check on you,' Cesare said quietly. 'She was worried about you.'

'She loves me.' His voice sounded strange, hoarse and half choked with the power of that intense emotion. 'She told me she loved me and I told her to walk away.'

'Sounds logical.' The words were oddly gentle. 'She's an amazing woman.'

'Yes,' he said simply. 'She is.' He looked up from the fallen tumbler and met his friend's gaze. 'You're right. I do love her.'

'Of course you do,' Cesare said and smiled. 'So now you're going to do what I did, which is try to be the husband she deserves and the father your children need. And if you fail, you try again and again and again.'

'Because she's important,' Aristophanes said roughly, the fire burning inside him, a fire he knew wasn't ever going to burn out. 'Because I can't live without her. Because she's worth it. She's worth everything.'

And she was, he knew that now. Which meant he couldn't let his fear guide him. Nell was having his children and she'd faced that with courage and strength. Faced him and his ridiculous demands with the same. She'd matched him will for will, and he knew now—perhaps too late—that in the end, for all his IQ points, it was she who was smarter than he was. She who was more perceptive, more brave, more honest, more compassionate.

Cesare was right. She was better than he was in every way and he couldn't live without her. He wouldn't.

Aristophanes shoved himself to his feet and stood there, swaying a little yet determined. Cesare also got up, putting a steadying hand on his shoulder. Then he frowned and sniffed theatrically. 'For God's sake, man,' he muttered. 'At least have a shower first before you go to her.'

Nell sat in the featureless hotel room, on the edge of the bed, staring down at the schedule in her hand. The schedule Aristophanes had given her when they'd arrived in London. Today was supposed to be a 'Nell's choice' day, yet the words made her eyes fill with tears.

There would be no choice today. Today was going to be filled with wondering what to do next and planning how she was going to cope. She didn't know how long it would last, him absenting himself. Would he contact her again? Would she ever even see him again? And what would happen with the children? What would she say to them?

So many unanswered questions. He'd told her to leave and she had. She'd gone to a hotel because she couldn't bear being at his Knightsbridge residence in case he came home. It hurt too much.

She had no idea what to do next.

A rush of sudden fury caught at her and she abruptly screwed up the schedule and threw the ball of paper at the nearest wall.

How dared he do this to her? How dared he abandon his children? How dared he leave her like this, weeping and feeling shattered in a featureless hotel room in a strange country?

How dared he make her fall in love with him and then tell her to walk away?

Stupid, *stupid* man!

Tears filled her eyes and she covered her face with her hands, allowing herself to weep for a little bit. Afterwards, she'd clean her face and have a shower. Get dressed and eat something. Then she'd try to figure out what the future looked like with twins if he refused to be a part of their little family, but until then, she was going to have a damn good cry.

There was a sudden, loud knock on the door.

Nell muttered a hoarse curse under her breath, grabbed some tissues from the table beside the bed and hurriedly wiped her eyes, before going to the door.

The knock came again, louder and more impatient sounding this time.

'Okay, okay,' she said tiredly, and, without bothering to check the peephole, pulled open the door.

Aristophanes stood in the doorway, his black hair standing up on end, no tie, his shirt crumpled. There was dark stubble on his jaw. He looked like hell. He was also the most beautiful sight she'd ever seen.

Her stomach dropped away, at the same time as her fury leapt high. 'What the bloody hell do you want?' she demanded. 'I thought you told me to leave.'

'I did.' His eyes were blazing silver, his voice rough with emotion. 'I was wrong.'

Nell's heart tightened. 'I don't know—'

'Let me in,' he said hoarsely. 'Please, Nell. Please let me in.'

She didn't want to and yet she found herself giving ground as he took a step forward and then another and another, backing her slowly into the hotel room, the door swinging shut behind them. Then he stopped and stared at her as if he hadn't seen her for years and years instead of only the night before.

Nell swallowed and folded her arms. She wasn't going to be the first one to speak.

'I was wrong,' he said starkly, obliging her. 'I shouldn't have asked you to leave. Because you're right, it *was* easier to make someone go than it is to ask them to stay. And I was just…terrified that I wasn't enough to make you stay. I'm a difficult man, Nell. I'm arrogant. I am not empathetic. And I do not like to be wrong.' His broad chest heaved as he sucked in a breath. 'I will make you a terrible husband and I hope to God I won't be a terrible father, and, quite frankly, that also terrifies me. I'm terrified of not being enough for you.'

He ran a hand through his hair. 'You're so amazing. You're a better person than I am in every way, smarter, braver, more honest. But… I want to try, Nell. I want to be worthy of you.' The look in his eyes blazed brighter. 'I'm in love with you and I don't know how this is supposed to work… All I know is that I can't live without you.'

There were more tears rolling down her cheeks. All her fury had died, vanished without a trace, leaving in its place something hot, something that felt suspiciously like joy.

He loved her. He really did. It was there, burning bright, in his eyes.

'You don't have to do anything to be worthy of me, Bear,' she said huskily. 'All you have to be is yourself, just as you are, arrogance, stubbornness, and difficult behaviours and all.'

He took another step towards her, and then one more, and then suddenly she was in his arms, held tight and close to his chest, his heat and his strength flowing into her. And something that had knotted tight and hard in her heart abruptly released, making her turn her face into his shirt to stem yet more tears that threatened.

'I love you,' he murmured into her hair. 'I can't live without you, Nell. Don't ever leave me, don't ever leave me again.'

She swallowed and lifted her head, staring up into his beautiful face. 'I won't. Not ever again.'

He bent and kissed her, and it went on for some time. Then she put her hands against his chest and said, laughing, 'You're very damp.'

'Cesare told me to have a shower before I came to you. I was too impatient to dry myself.'

She laughed. 'Idiot, Bear. Were you angry that I called him?'

'No.' He kissed her again, hungrier this time. 'I was glad. He can be very intelligent sometimes.' Another hot kiss, then he lifted his head, looking down at her, one hand curving possessively over her stomach. 'Nell, I know you didn't choose to be the mother of my children, but I would very much like it if you chose to be my wife.'

Her heart was full, a joy she'd never thought would ever be hers making a home for itself inside her. Making a home for him, too, and their babies. A family, together.

'Yes, Bear,' she said, smiling. 'Yes, I think I'd like that very much, too.'

# EPILOGUE

'TWINS,' CESARE SAID through gritted teeth, as five children caused havoc in Aristophanes' previously immaculate pool area, 'are such a delight.'

Someone screeched, and there was a splash, followed by a howl of accusation.

'That's your son, I believe,' Lark murmured from the sun lounger, not looking up from her book.

Aristophanes tried not to smile as Cesare rolled his eyes, got up from his lounger, and went to deal with the offender. Then Aristophanes surreptitiously checked on Plato and Hypatia to make sure it wasn't either of his children causing the drama, since they were known mischief-makers. But it seemed not to be the case now, as they were playing an innocent game at the other end of the pool. A suspiciously innocent game.

Idly, he wondered if he should go and do something about it, then decided not to. He was enjoying sitting here, watching over the children with Cesare and Lark.

They'd come for a week's visit with their three children, filling his house with chaos and noise and laughter and happiness.

In fact, he wasn't sure he could get any happier. His

life had become the most glorious thing. He was no longer tied to his schedule. He simply didn't need it any more. He knew what was important, and that was his wife and his children, and while his business had to be managed, he'd decided to delegate that to someone else, at least until the children were older. He hadn't regretted it.

After the twins had been born, Nell had decided to take a job at the charity the fundraiser they'd attended had been in aid of, which she did remotely. Because she too knew what was important. Then again, she'd always known that.

Thinking of Nell, he wondered where she'd got to. She'd gone into the house, muttering something about peace and quiet, and hadn't come out again.

'I'm going to check on Nell,' he murmured to Lark. 'Can you keep an eye on—?'

'Of course,' she said, still not looking up from her book. 'Cesare! Watch Hy and Plato for a minute!'

Aristophanes grinned as he got up from his lounger while his friend gave him a long-suffering look from the side of the pool. All a front, as Aristophanes well knew. Cesare loved watching the kids.

He stepped into the cool of the salon just as Nell came through from the hallway. She wore a white dress and her hair was loose and flowing over her shoulders, and desire hit him hard in the gut, the way it always did.

His beautiful, amazing wife.

He reached out to her and she came over, taking his hand and lacing her fingers through his. 'Where did you go?' he asked. 'I missed you.'

She looked up at him, her dark eyes sparkling. 'I have something to tell you.'

Aristophanes raised her hand to his mouth and kissed it. 'Oh?'

'Do you think we could do another philosopher name? Or is three in the family too much?'

His heart leapt. 'Nell...'

'Because if it's a girl, I like Theodora,' Nell went on. 'And if it's a boy, I was thinking maybe Aristotle—'

But she never got to finish, because Aristophanes had pulled her close and was now kissing her hungrily.

He'd been wrong after all.

It was perfectly possible for his life to get even happier.

\* \* \* \* \*

*Did you fall head over heels for*
The Twins That Bind*?*
*Then you're sure to adore the first instalment in*
*the Scandalous Heirs duet*
'Italian Baby Shock*!*

*And don't miss these other Jackie Ashenden stories!*

Pregnant with Her Royal Boss's Baby
His Innocent Unwrapped in Iceland
A Vow to Redeem the Greek
Enemies at the Greek Altar
Spanish Marriage Solution

*Available now!*

# HARLEQUIN
### Reader Service

# Enjoyed your book?

Try the perfect subscription for Romance readers and get more great books like this delivered right to your door.

See why over 10+ million readers have tried Harlequin Reader Service.

## Start with a Free Welcome Collection with free books and a gift—valued over $20.

Choose any series in print or ebook.
See website for details and order today:

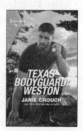

## TryReaderService.com/subscriptions